NOTHING SIMPLE

OR EASY

Mark T. Sneed

ISBN: 978-0-578-80375-3

DEDICATION

To my mother, family and friends who continue to inspire, encourage and challenge me to be a better and more loving person.

THANK YOU

All those who have loved and lost, loved from afar, longed
for love and been too shy, too loud, too short, too tall, too
thin or too fat. Thank you. You inspire me to open my heart
to the possibilities and dreams of unconditional love even
in a seemingly endless dark world. I am encouraged to keep
searching for my queen.

Table of Contents

Chapter One 1

Chapter Two.. 21

Chapter Three... 45

Chapter Four.. 57

Chapter Five.. 81

Chapter Six... 109

Chapter Seven 121

Chapter Eight.. 131

Chapter Nine 147

Chapter Ten 157

Chapter Eleven 173

Chapter Twelve.. 183

Chapter Thirteen 197

Chapter Fourteen 209

Chapter One

Jules Semple was not a criminal. He was not a gangster. He was not a thug. He did not run drugs. Yet, every day he walked the streets of Chicago dressed in a hoodie or a suit he was a potential criminal to all the police.

Was it Jules Semple's fault he was nearly six-foot-two-inches-tall and two hundred pounds of dark chocolate and unafraid to walk down the most dangerous streets in Chicago? He never looked for or instigated trouble. He was blessed with his size, strength and being unafraid, perhaps it was genetics.

His mother was tall for a woman. She was five foot eight inches tall. His mother said that his father was tall as well. Jules did not know. He had grown up an only child with just his mother. His biological father vanished shortly after he was born and lived in the neighborhood, according to some who knew the streets of the one-time second city.

Jules had grown up on the westside of Chicago and seen pimps, pushers, gangsters and drug dealers and the girls who gravitated around the powerful men in the street. Jules, big and quiet, had never been recruited by the local gangs as most thought he was associated with a gang because he hung out with several gang members. Tre and Harold, New Breeds and Black Disciples respectively, were from rival gangs but they had grown up with Jules. Jules had avoided any real gang affiliation thanks to Tre and Harold.

He, at sixteen, had decided to play football. He wanted to be a running back but was too slow. His high school football coach, upon seeing him, though he had only played touch football in the neighborhood prior, placed him as a tight end. Jules had great hands and impressed his coaches with his tenacity.

Jules scored nearly one hundred touchdowns in three years. By his senior year Jules was being looked at by several smaller colleges in Illinois, Indiana, Michigan and Ohio. Jules was good but not good enough to garner the attention of the University of Illinois, Indiana State, Michigan State University, or Ohio State University. The biggest school to recruit Jules was Northwestern University.

Jules got an athletic scholarship. He also got a handful of scholastic scholarships. Despite the scholarships he struggled with the decision to go to college. He did not want to leave his mother alone. So, Jules had stayed close to home. He had attended Elmhurst college and once there played rugby instead of football.

At Elmhurst college he met Max a bright and intelligent young man with aspirations of working as a vice-president or assistant to a president at his father's accounting firm. He was fascinated by numbers and money, and his family was couched in market shares, bottom lines and fiscal reports. His father was one of vice presidents for one of the biggest Chicago financial firms.

Although Jules worked for the Chicago Tribune, he was not a reporter, nor a photographer. He worked in the technology department. Jules used his scholarships to get a degree in computer technology. He had become fascinated by computers in college. That led him to working at the Tribune. He found his work surprisingly fun and interesting.

He was one of a dozen guys at the Tribune who worked to keep the reporter's technology up to date. Jules was one of a hundred guys who exited the train just a few blocks from Michigan Avenue and descended the stairs everyday just a stone's throw from the Chicago River. He and hundreds of others walked to the Magnificent Mile and turned left to see the iconic Wrigley Building on one side of the street. Jules and hundreds crossed Michigan Avenue and streamed into the other icon on the avenue known simply as the Tribune Building.

Jules loved the fact he worked downtown. It was a privilege to work in the Tribune building. He had been given a Chicago Tribune badge when he first started and been so proud to show it to Harold and Tre.

"Check you out," Tre laughed.

"You taking over for Herb Caan? Or Siskel?"

"I'm not a reporter," Jules said.

"You doing computer stuff?" Harold asked, shaking his head.

Jules Semple had come back to college and moved his mother out of the small two-bedroom apartment on the westside and into a spacious and safe two-bedroom in a brick front building in Oak Park, just a few minutes from downtown Chicago.

Interested in living close to his mother but yearning for his own independence he compromised. He found a little apartment in Logan Square, just a train or bus ride from his mom. Logan Square was close to downtown Chicago. It was a surprisingly eclectic neighborhood and one where Jules enjoyed his independent life.

Jules smiled at his achievements. He walked into the lobby and to the elevator banks where an entrance was secured by two men in front of a metal detector. At a counter sat a woman with a notebook computer.

Jules scanned his badge every day he arrived and every day he left. The Chicago Tribune newspaper was spread out across the top half of the twenty-story building. The bottom half of the Tribune had been sold to various commercial offices.

One the eleventh floor of the Tribune building Jules and the computer team gathered behind a keyless secured door in the technology department and listen to D'Angelo Wendell, the chief of technology. Wendell daily discussed the various issues in the Tribune building. Bobby Turner and Vincent Roman were good friends of Jules. Bobby Turner was a techno nerd. He was given the responsibility of server maintenance. Vincent Roman, a Northwestern University graduate, was a tall square faced individual with a high forehead and moustache and goatee. He looked like a throwback to the three-piece suit wearing seventies porn star.

Jules liked working at the Chicago Tribune. He had been at the Tribune for nearly half a decade. He was tasked with the maintenance of eight departments. Jules was responsible for Advertising, Obituaries, Jobs & Work, Classified, Real Estate, Autos, Breaking News and Tribune Archives.

Everyday Jules sat at his desk, a dozen floors below the reporters creating innovative, informative and investigative stories which mattered to the Chicagoland and surrounding cities, while he put out technical issues which came from a working staff of over seven hundred people.

Jules loved his job. Every day he came to work he never knew what he might face. It excited him. The work challenged him.

While he worked at the Chicago Tribune he focused only on the work. For Jules, unraveling the technological knots tied by employees satisfied him. He was responsible for technology maintenance and monitoring of Horoscopes, Puzzles and Games and Public Notices. For some reason the small and witchy team in the Horoscopes daily threatened to infect the entire Tribune network with malware. One of Jules greatest achievements was the creation of a network within a network to quarantine the troubled departments which seemed prone to malware.

"How do you teach people not to click the links on emails of people they don't know?" Bobby Turner asked. He was a small shouldered tall drink of water who liked to wear collared shirts, blue jeans and Nike tennis shoes. In all the time Jules knew Bobby, he never saw him wear the same shoes once.

Jules wished for the biggest issue in his life being the shoes he was going to wear the next day, like Bobby Turner. According to his friends he had bigger problems than shoes.

"Jules you are a relatively non-hideous semi-bright individual," Max said. "You should not be at home alone."

"Come on man, you can't be satisfied without a honey next to you," Bobby Turner said.

No matter what Jules said his friends pointed to the fact he was alone. Jules sometimes dreaded the inevitable questions and invitations. He dreamed of simple shoe problems.

Jules tried to deflect his college friends, his neighborhood friends and work friends concern about his lack of a personal life. Max was blunt and direct. That was Max's style. Harold and Tee were subtle. They poked and prodded but in a nonverbal kind of way. They would pick him up and there were always two girls in the car who were unattached.

Perhaps it is how Jules had gotten roped into going out with friends and trying to be a little hipper than usual. Max had begged him, and he had agreed. Perhaps, he thought absently, it was what had led to him to being locked in the trunk of a car, in downtown Chicago, going God knows where.

He had been bum rushed from the club by Diamond Martin and three of his thuggish crew. Jules, once outside the club and on the streets of Lower Wacker Drive, thought there might be a hand-to-hand fight between him and Diamond or one of his Freakyville Rogers Park crew.

There were four against one. The odds were not the greatest, but Jules did not shrink from the upcoming fight, be it against Diamond or all. Jules, dressed in a slim fit long sleeved floral shirt, black trousers, comfortable black leather lace-up dress boots, and a leather belt, prepared to knuckle up.

"Cole, take this overstepping piece of shit out of my sight," Diamond Martin said.

The three Rogers Park thugs circled him. One reached out and Jules knew it was a fishing expedition. He eyed the three thugs in front of him, circling him, and measured his opponents. There was the leader Diamond dressed all flashy, but he was not the real threat. He was dangerous, no question. Yet, it was the long-faced thug Cole, who Jules concentrated on, who was the biggest danger. He was the one Jules imagined to be the most unpredictable.

Jules hesitated, knowing most dust ups in Chicago ended one of three ways: one, the two funking parties walked away unsatisfied; two, the two funking parties got beaten up and one was a winner and the other lost; third, and most common, one of the two funking parties pulled a gat and started capping.

There was two of Diamond Martin's henchmen. There was a big boy with a tight fade, wearing a leather jacket, silk collared shirt, baggy jeans and Nike Jordans. Next to him stood a gap-toothed peanut headed brother wearing a jean jacket, T-shirt and baggy blue jeans. Jules looked at the long-faced Cole. He looked like the one ready to pull the cannon. Jules estimated of the Rogers Park crew Cole might be the first to pull a hand cannon and end it all.

The three rushed him and Jules reluctantly allowed the Freakyville crew to rough him up, just a little, to prove a point and when he expected the pushing and shoving to end, they dragged him to their car.

"What gives?" Semple asked and as an answer he had been clipped behind the ear and woken up in the trunk of a car.

Jules twisted and turned in the closeness of the dark trunk and thought over his life. The brake lights flashed, and Jules attempted to find the latch on the trunk to release him. He fumbled and the red lights illuminated the trunk briefly faded.

The darkness made Jules again reflect on his life. His brother and sister were out of the house when he went to high school. He had talked to a few girls and had a girlfriend here and there but nothing too serious. In his four years in high school, he had kissed a girl twice. He had gone to his Junior prom and skipped the Senior prom.

He was not a lady's man. He was friendly enough but when it came time for picking and choosing Jules usually just went home. Jules just found the whole game of chase annoying and unpalatable.

Jules had, in his twenty-five years of life, only two girlfriends. Girlfriends, by Jules' definition, were girls who allowed him to see them naked. Before his two girlfriends Jules had been friends with a number of girls he had kissed and hugged but nothing more.

The two girls, Katlyn and Vivian, had been weeks of strain and discomfort for Jules. They seemed to need so much. Jules never seemed to be able to satisfy them. Eventually, they had broken off their relations off with Jules. They detailed in no uncertain terms the reason for the breakup. No matter what, Jules realized, it was his fault one hundred percent of the time.

He had met Katlyn at a park near his college apartment his sophomore year at Elmhurst. She was this firebrand of a girl the color of maple syrup and with big brown eyes and a big personality. Kathleen Thomas liked Jules because he was quiet. The end of his first relationship came when Kathleen started flirting with another boy just to get a rise out of Jules. Jules did not bite on the baiting. He had learned not to fight over a girl. That was the end of his first real girlfriend experience. It had lasted for just under a month. He was nearly twenty when Katlyn said things were over.

There were warnings. Katlyn seemed to want more than Jules.

"You are emotionally absent," Katlyn said as if in so saying it would hurt Jules' feelings.

The end of that relationship was not what Jules expected. Katlyn had decided one night, a Thursday night, things were over.

"I don't think that you care about me," Katlyn had said. He was still living in Elmhurst, near the college. "I just think that it would be better if we stopped seeing each other."

That was it. The end of his first real college relationship. It, the end of that relationship, did not seem to have any gravity or impact on Jules. He had agreed and though he did not see or call Kathleen it, her absence, was not notable. That lack of notice did not seem too big a deal.

Jules had studied and gotten more and more into computer science and computer systems while at Elmhurst and suddenly he was preparing to graduate. He had become friends with Max and a handful of others while at Elmhurst but never found the Elmhurst girls attractive or interesting enough to expend any energy on them.

Max was dating Lorraine at the time and introduced Jules to Vivian.

"You'll like her," Max promised. "She's nice."

The second relationship he had was two months ago and nearly five years after Jules had left college. The introduction had come through Max. Jules had tried to avoid the meeting. Her name was Vivian Godfrey. She was this angular white girl with long brown hair and an athletic body. She was a good soccer player at Elmhurst College. Jules did not dislike Vivian. He just did not find her electric.

"Give it time," Max advised.

Jules had gone out with Vivian a few things and Vivian was fun. She seemed driven. Vivian lived in Brookfield. Her family had money. Vivian wanted to work in international security for some reason. Her father was a big deal businessman, she told Jules. Jules learned the soccer player had issues with her daddy. She was getting back at her father going out with Jules.

"I don't really care how you get back at your daddy," Jules admitted after a sexual romp with the pliable Vivian Godfrey.

"What? Don't you care that my daddy doesn't want to meet you?" Vivian asked.

"No, not really," Jules had admitted.

Like Katlyn and Vivian seemed to know what they wanted. Katlyn sought Jules out. Vivian after meeting Jules would just show up at his college apartment. But as quickly as the relations had begun the relations had ended. Vivian, a free spirit, complained over and over of Jules inability to show emotions.

"I'm alive, Vivian, I don't perform, like some circus entertainer," Jules recalled saying. "I have emotions, but they are not triggered by you and your need for me to show you something."

"Are you sure? Are you really that in control of your emotions? Are you? Or are you just emotionally cut off?" Vivian when angry was cutthroat. The arguments could become emotional bloodbaths, Jules recalled.

"If you are really alive, you are not able to express your emotions." Vivian constantly challenged Jules and his locked-up emotions. "You don't seem like you are happy. It seems that when you want to jump my bones you are into it, but then after you don't care." Vivian said. "If I just wanted a friend with benefits, I wouldn't put up with all this."

Vivian, ever the lady, went so far as to question his desires. Jules had laughed at the idea. He loved girls. He did not just like them.

The problem was...he did not like Vivian or any of the girls he had met danced with, kissed and hugged more than in passing. When he saw them, he was courteous and not rude. When they were not around, he did not think about any of them anymore.

His relationship with Vivian ended as unexpectedly as it had begun.

Max, his closest college friend, had tried to salvage the relationship between Jules and Vivian while he was working at the Tribune.

"Jules, we're working and trying to solidify a few things," Max begun, months ago in Jules' mind. Three weeks ago, Jules recalled. "We are starting our lives and get jobs and figuring shit out. You don't want to do that on your own. You want to have someone who has your back. Vivian is a good person."

"Max, me and Vivian are not going to work," Jules had told his friend and like a good friend that was enough. "She has too many daddy issues and I am not going to play the spoiler or give the old man a heart attack to make Vivian happy."

Max understood. "Fuck her then," Max concluded.

A few weeks later Jules and Max had gotten drunk the night Jules told Max Vivian had broken up with him. Max had driven them out of the city and back to Elmhurst and back to a college bar near the campus. The two college friends sat in the bar and Max tried to make Jules feel better.

"I'm not sad," Jules said.

"You are sad. Everyone gets sad when you get dumped," Max said.

"I'm not sad," Jules said.

Max ordered drinks. The two college friends drank. They drank lots. Drunk and stupidly giddy Jules and Max celebrated the end of Jules' latest relationship. In that drunken night Max had said one thing which stuck with Jules.

"You know figuring out who we are takes a lifetime?" Max said as they left the bar and sat on the edge of the quiet Elmhurst lake in the middle of the college night three years ago. Jules agreed. "What happens in between that figuring is what we call life."

Max was bright and incredibly intelligent. He had been undeclared when he arrived at Elmhurst and studied a dozen subjects before settling on Economics. That night he was sloppy drunk and blinking in and out of brilliance and seeming borderline vaudeville comedy.

Jules took the train back into the city and left Max in Elmhurst. On the train ride back to Chicago Jules realized he secretly wished he could find someone who he wanted to be with not just for a moment. He did not want to be alone. Yet, he did not want to be with someone because he was lonely. That was not fair to the person who he was with.

The problem was like Katlyn and probably Vivian to some extent, he had no idea of what he wanted. He did not know himself. What Jules did know was he did not understand the reason he had been with Katlyn or Vivian. Maybe, Jules' thought, he was uncaring. He did not seem interested in the things his friends were interested in. Jules had to admit neither of his two grown relationships were passionate affairs by any stretch of the imagination.

That Friday night, a few days after Vivian broke up with Jules, Max took him out to get his mind off things and Jules against his better thoughts decided to do something different. Doing something different lead him to new ground.

It had ended with Jules in the trunk of a car. There was loud brassy music washing over him as the car raced in some unknown direction. Jules Semple would have laughed at the fact for a quarter of a century he had chosen not to color outside of the lines and in one night, one errant remark, one look, one five-minute talk he found himself locked in a car trunk.

The car turned and jostled Jules. He tried to unlock the trunk and found the car, whichever it was, did not have the childproof trunk latch. Jules closed his eyes and tried to imagine how he had gotten tossed in the back of a car's trunk. He tried for a couple of more minutes and realized that he was locked in the trunk of a car and being driven God knows where.

Semple felt the knot rising on the back of his head and immediately recalled Diamond and his thugs had been upset he had dared talk to the long-legged Bethany. It seemed everyone except Semple knew Bethany was Diamond's girl. For the insult Diamond and the Freakyville crew decided to teach Semple a lesson.

Instantly, his thoughts went to: Was he going to be killed? People had died for less, Jules knew. The car made a hard left and then right and jerked to a stop. As he weighed his odds of making it out of the predicament, he was in he heard the muffled voices of several people in the car. Semple prepared for the worse.

The trunk opened and the long-faced thug was wearing a thick gold chain around his neck who went by Cole, smiled down on Semple.

Semple hesitated as Cole leaned down holding a gun effortlessly in his right hand. Two others Jules did not know reached in and grabbed Semple. Semple struggled against the rough grappling and cuffing as the two thugs; one a peanut hued, small shouldered kid wearing a bright silk shirt without collar and a belt buckle which looked like it had been won in a rodeo, and the other a bird beaked boy with bushy eyebrows and a grimace on his chocolate brown face who was wearing a black collared shirt, baggy designer jeans and a pinky ring.

Once out of the trunk and in the grips of peanut boy and the bird beaked thug Semple found himself dragged a few feet on the always busy lower Wacker Drive. Jules was sure he was on the lower Wacker Drive but exactly where was a mystery.

The club was near the entrance to lower Wacker Drive in an abandoned pizza shop. There was a cross street and a traffic light Jules recalled near the club. He looked back and forth and noticed they were in a space in between the dim lights of lower Wacker

Drive where a dozen cars were parked. The main street was behind Diamond. Jules looked back and saw the Dearborn Bridge in the distance to the right.

After a short struggle and Cole grabbing Jules by the collar, he was again face-to-face with Diamond Martin, Freakyville drug boy and psychopath. Jules' arms were behind his back, held firm by the two thugs who had pulled him from the car trunk. Cole was closest to Semple.

"So, you think you can waltz into my club and talk with my girl and there not by any consequences for something like that?"

Semple smiled. He smiled because he had been surprised that Diamond had used the word: consequences. Perhaps, he underestimated Diamond Martin. Before Semple could remove the smile, he felt a slight smack on the back of his head from one of the thugs.

The smack was a reminder Jules was an unwelcome prisoner, against his will, and the only way he could liberate himself was to knuckle up and fight with the four thugs, including one with a gun. Jules closed his eyes to the smack, not because it hurt but because he had to decide then and there how he was going to deal with this present situation.

"Answer the man when he talks to you," Cole growled.

Semple gave the peanut boy a side glance and looked at the long face of Cole and his gun in his right hand and thought long and hard about breaking away from the two thugs and shoving the gun down Cole's throat. Of course, shoving the gun down the thug's throat would leave Jules unarmed against the remaining three thugs.

He blinked and rethought the attack, if he was going to attack.

He would have to disarm Cole first or risk the long-faced thug getting off a lucky shot and hitting or killing Jules before he could do anything. Cole was the first-person Jules had to attack. The peanut boy and the bird boy, though they held him, were the secondary targets. Then there was Diamond Martin.

Jules considered the idea of fighting his way out of his situation but, at the moment, the odds were long and not in his favor. So, Jules took a deep breath. He had to play the odds. Maybe, he was not destined to die that day.

Out of the corner of his eye Semple saw Cole grimace and the peanut boy raise his hand again.

"I didn't know she was your girl," Semple said, rethinking the possibility of shoving the gun down Cole's throat. Peanut boy grinned, showing a mouthful of gold teeth. Bird boy just shook his head. Cole chuckled and bird boy looked from Diamond back to the peanut boy, who lowered his hand, and back to Diamond.

"Everybody knows that Bee is my girl," Diamond smiled, showing off his four gold incisors.

"Well, not everybody," Semple smiled. "I didn't."

Cole reached out and introduced Jules to the butt of his gun.

Jules winced. He looked at Cole chillingly. Cole smiled and shook his head, holding his gun all sideways like in the gangster movies.

"Where you from?"

Semple hated the question. In Chicago, in most neighborhoods he walked through or drove through or traveled through the question wasn't an informal question. It was a question of loyalty. It was a query of heart, soul and mind. It was a question which answered so much in its response Semple knew he had to be cautious. People died answering the question incorrectly. People had been beaten saying the wrong thing to what Diamond Martin was asking with one thug holding a gun and two others restraining Semple.

"Answer the man, when he asks you a question, bitch ass nigger," Cole hissed. Cole was the color of polished oak wood and wiry and dressed like a thug going to a party. He had on Timberland boots, oversized denim pants, no belt, some gawdy designer shirt and matching gawdy designer sweatshirt. On his wrist was an incredibly expensive wristwatch. He had short, cropped hair and an earring in his ear.

They were downtown. They were on Wacker Drive, Semple thought. They were some Freakyville Rogers Park hard hitters, according to the bartender of the pop-up club, Semple recalled. He had a couple of cousins who lived up north and in the twenty-five years he had lived in Chicago he had visited them three times. Semple had a strong dislike for the neighborhoods he did not know or live in, especially neighborhoods which spawned these upper northside bad boys. Jules took a gamble. There was no way it could end peaceably, anyway.

"I'm from the West," Simple said.

"Westside, nigger," Diamond scowled. "Figures."

Then and there, Semple thought his life was over. He just was waiting for Diamond or Cole to step to Jules and place the gun against his chest and pull the trigger. The hate between the westside and Rogers Park was intense.

Rogers Park and westside did not get along. Southside did not like the westside. There was a long-time rift between the westside and the two other sides of Chicago for as long as blacks lived in Chicago.

"Nigger, I see you again, this ends differently." Diamond Martin sneered. He was being magnanimous. The Rogers Park leader, turned to Cole and said: "Toss that nigger in the river and see if he drown like a rat or swim like a dog."

Cole snapped the gun in front of Jules' face and peanut boy and bird boy instantly pulled Jules by the arms backward and spun him around. They dragged him toward the railing of lower Wacker Drive.

"Should we strip this nigger?" The peanut boy asked. Jules slowed and peanut boy and bird beak had to push just a little harder.

"Naw, this just a warning," Diamond said. "Next time we see this bitch then all bets are off," the Freakyville thug announced.

Peanut boy nodded and as he pushed Jules forward the computer technician felt his watch being slipped off his wrist. Jules smirked. He looked at the peanut boy coolly.

"What nigger, you going to cry?" Peanut boy growled close to Jules' ear. Peanut boy had his hair in cornrows. He had a diamond stud in his ear. He had a gold chain with an eagle head on it. On his right hand were the letters that made up: Hate. Jules committed those details to memory.

Bird boy tapped on Jules' ass a couple of times. Jules turned his gaze at him.

"What nigger?" The darker of the two henchmen growled. Jules wanted to laugh at the comedy of the situation. The dark bird boy was a little fruity, Jules mused. He studied bird boy as the two laughed and cackled like hyenas. Bird boy was the color of burnt sienna and had a knife scar across his chin. He had an oval face and thin eyes. Jules noted he also had a gold chain around his neck. He also had the stupidly obnoxious gold pinky ring. The most distinct feature about bird boy, to Jules was his hooked nose. Bird boy could have easily been called Toucan Sam in Jules' book without hesitation. As he pushed Jules' forward Jules felt him feeling him up. Jules wanted to say something but at the moment the disrespectful action was low on the priority list of egregious actions needed to be redressed.

The thief and the soft boy dragged Jules to the edge of the retaining wall and barrier to the lower part of Wacker Drive with Cole holding his gun on Jules. Cole seemed to be enjoying the humiliation the most. He could not stop himself from laughing and smiling at Jules' predicament as he walked beside Jules.

"You ain't going to scream, nigger?"

"No, man, ain't no need to scream," Jules said. "It's just water."

Cole stopped at Jules' words.

Jules looked at Cole and back toward the low wall which was only three or four feet high. At two o'clock in the morning there were few lights on the river. Jules tried to look across the river and see if there was anyone who might help him.

He looked back at Cole.

"Dude's crazy, Cole," peanut boy hissed.

"Yeah, let's just dunk him and go," bird beak boy chirped. He had hold of Jules' left wrist.

Cole regained his composure and narrowed his dark brown

eyes.

"You lucky that Diamond just wants you wet," Cole said. "If it was up to me, I'd drop you right here."

Jules looked at Cole and believed it. Cole looked like one of those hard hitters that had to constantly prove to himself that he was hard. He studied Cole and based on a cursory glance knew he was high on something. He had recalled Cole had a couple of drinks. Maybe, Jules imagined, Cole was a mean drunk.

None of that mattered. They were now at the retaining wall. Jules stuck his foot out and onto the retaining wall to brace himself.

The two who had pushed and prodded him to that point for the first time felt Jules give a little resistance.

"You scared, nigger?" Cole sneered.

Cole put the barrel of the gun to the back of Jules' head.

"You go for a swim or go to the morgue," Cole threatened.

Jules shook the two thugs off and stepped up and over the retaining wall. He looked back and was about to say something when Diamond Martin, appeared out of nowhere and kicked Jules as hard as he could in the stomach to drive him backwards and into the space between Lower Wacker Drive and the Chicago River.

Chapter *Two*

Parker loved Chicago. He had been in the city all his life. He had been born in the Cook County Hospital nearly six decades ago. He was a dark man, the color of ground coffee. He had a salt and pepper uncut moustache and beard which hid his mouth. His hair was an uncombed swirl of gray which looked more like cotton candy than hair. It was obvious, at first sight, Kenneth Parker did not concern himself with his appearance. He was just trying to survive another winter. To survive, he slept in his barely functioning van parked illegally in one of the Chicago Department of Transportation businesses which had taken sympathy on him and allowed him to park his van there. Parker climbed out of the vehicle which held all his valuables and slowly made his way to the decrepit pier, where he played his saxophone late at night.

Parker, what everyone called him, walked out toward the pier and the cautionary signs, long after everyone in the CDOT workshop had left and the city started to welcome the night.

He did not wear a watch. There was no reason to care about time. He had not punched a clock in years. All Parker knew was he slept until he woke. He might scrounge some food dumpster diving near the State Street restaurants. He would return to the CDOT parking lot and just before they locked up for the night sleep a little more.

Parker had woken and found all the lights out in the CDOT building where the parking lot sat were the three CDOT trucks parked beside Parker's van. In the small parking lot Parker looked at the three trucks and then to the workshop. He fished out a piece of food that might have been a piece of steak or jerky and tossed the strip into his salt and pepper beard. He wiped his hand on his tattered trench coat and patted Bessie, his prized saxophone. Dressed in a tatty hat and olive-green trench coat Parker moved slowly to the disused pier. Parker walked gingerly, favoring his left leg, toward the crumbling pier.

He picked his way across the broken and disintegrating pier and sat on a broken chair near the edge of the river and wet his lips. From his trench coat Parker pulled a silver flask that he opened and sipped. Carefully, Parker replaced the flask and hoisted Bessie up and into his hands. He fingered the keys and smiled. It was in that moment Parker transformed.

All the troubles of the world coming down upon him fell away as he put his lips to the mouthpiece and breathed life into Bessie. The air, from Parker's lungs was pushed through the mouthpiece and into the inner workings of the inanimate object which was to many just a gold alto sax but with a welcoming breath and Parker's fingering of the silver keys Bessie came to life.

Bessie yawned and stretched and in the hands of Parker the yawning and stretching. Bessie issued her first notes of the night. Parker breathed and let Bessie speak the notes within her. She was a naughty and devilish girl, Parker noted as he fingered the keys and Bessie toyed with the music he was playing.

The saxophonist did not rush Bessie. He held her gently and played one of the first songs he had learned to play long ago in high school. The song was a jazzy number which touched everyone's heart anytime he played it. Henry Mancini's Pink Panther came to life. From Pink Panther Parker played another popular ditty, Tequila. He was feeling good and attempted Careless Whisper but did not hit all the notes like he had the two previous tunes. Parker redoubled his efforts and played a particularly poignant song from his repertoire he had been working on for months. Bessie and Parker breathed an old song by Little Willie John called: Need Your Love So Bad.

The gray-haired Parker was not paying attention to time; he never did when he and Bessie were on the pier and filling the silence up with the sounds of times gone by time became meaningless. Yet, as Parker played "Need Your Love So Bad" he felt the music transcend his breathing and fingering. It was as if Bessie and Parker were one. His breathing and fingering, at the particular moment, was rhythmic and in sync with Bessie's cries and moans which echoed the sadness of Little Willie John in his long-ago appeal for love and acknowledgement.

Parker sat on the pier and played, trying to hold onto the feeling for as long as possible. The old man smiled as he played. He was happy. He was content, at peace and connected as he played Bessie.

As Parker was just finishing Little Willie John's song when he looked down and noticed there was a body fully dressed moving in the Chicago River. The body was of a big black man wearing a black and white floral shirt. For an instance, Parker thought his hooch was a little stronger than his regular favorite.

Parker stopped playing Bessie and looked closer. He believed he had imagined someone swimming in the Chicago River. No one swam in the Chicago River. No one.

Then Parker saw the brown face moving in the dark water toward the rotting pier. Parker cradled his saxophone and leaned forward and watched as the swimmer reached out and grabbed the pier's piling. Parker did not assist. He was unsure suddenly what to do. Parker watched as a hand reached out of the water and grabbed the pier's post.

Parker stood up, still holding his saxophone and watched as the man lifted himself out of the river and onto the rotting pier.

Parker twisted his lips, thinking. He was too old to run. Well, he was too feeble to run, he thought. If he ran, Parker thought, where would he go? The CDOT had locked the gate and there was no way he could climb over the ten-foot height without assistance. Mockingly, Parker thought, maybe he could ask the stranger to help him over the fence?

All his fears and worries disappeared once the stranger had

gotten atop the pier. Instead of the stranger attacking him or anything he simply lay on the dock breathing in as much air as he could like a fish might after jumping out of an aquarium.

Parker looked back at the man lying on the pier on his back-dripping river water everywhere. Would the river rat try to rob Parker? All he had that mattered was on him of value was Bessie. Parker did a mental check and knew he had a knife to protect himself on the pier from river rats. The knife was not very sharp or menacing. It was one of those utility knives with a screwdriver, tweezers and can opener attached. River rats were annoying but not a threat. Parker thought the river swimmer might be crazy if not an out-and-out threat.

If this goes sideways, Parker thought, I suppose I could bash in his brains with Bessie. The thought seemed inconceivable to the saxophonist. If worse comes to worse, he restated in his own head, he would have to fight the river rat with his utility knife.

Why would the man be a threat, Parker chided himself? Just because he was black? Just because he came out of the Chicago River alive. The saxophonist stopped himself. The man on the pier breathing in air like one of those fish jumping out of a tank was probably crazy. Anyone crazy enough to swim in the Chicago River had to be crazy, Parker decided.

He changed his thinking on the man just a few feet away from Parker's foot. The man was crazy, Parker rationalized. Crazy and alive. The man would be grateful to be alive, Parker thought.

Parker shook his head at his foolishness. There was never anyone swimming in the Chicago River. That was crazy. The Chicago River was the place where the dead were deposited. It was not a place to swim. Parker's thoughts were interrupted by the chocolate hand grabbing a hold of the pier. Parker sat Bessie down and watched curiously as things developed just a few feet from him.

The stranger, who had been in the river, lay on the pier for a full minute just breathing and dripping water everywhere. He sat up and seemed muscular but not from the gym, Parker thought absently. The man was big, the saxophonist realized. Maybe he was six-foot or six-foot two, Parker estimated. He was dressed in the long sleeve white and black floral shirt, black trousers and black lace-up boots.

The man sat in the darkness silently and turned to Parker. Parker noted the black man had a small cut over his left eyebrow. He was handsome in a Sidney Poitier kind of way. He had a broad nose and flat features as he sat on the pier catching his breath.

"Was she worth it?"

Jules opened and closed his eyes to the questions. He looked at the night sky above him. Water dripped off of him.

He looked right and took in the broken pier post and pier he had swam toward. In the darkness Jules was sure he saw two beady eyes looking at him. He could not concern himself with those two beady eyes. That was not his biggest issue. He looked left and saw the combat boot, the camouflage pants and edge of a trench coat. He looked up and there was the dark face of a man crowned with a gray uncombed crown of hair and a scraggly beard.

The man, a shambling mound of camouflage, gray, black and green, sat on his broken chair, looking at Jules like a teacher might a wayward student. The gray-haired man had a golden saxophone on his lap.

"You know, I've seen some crazy things come out of that there river, man. But, have to admit," Parker sang. "This is the first time I done seen a man come out it under his own steam."

Jules stretched his shoulders and lifted his arms up slowly, after catching his breath. The two men, one old and one young, were only a few feet apart. Yet, they are a million miles apart in terms of experience.

Parker leaned down and placed Bessie back in her case.

"You got a name?"

"Jules," Jules smiled, awkwardly and embarrassed.

The saxophonist nodded.

"I asked earlier, when you climbed out: Was she worth it?" Parker asked again, studying Jules.

Jules did not answer immediately. Instead, he wiped his face and looked around and tried to determine where he was on the river. He knew he was no longer near the Dearborn Bridge. He was all turned around.

"Maybe I made a mistake," Jules said more to himself than to Parker.

"What kind of mistake?"

Jules was surprised the old man had heard him. He blinked and squeezed at his nose and let some water drain away from his face before speaking.

"Went to a club tonight, last night, whatever, and tried doing things I should not have been doing," Jules tried to explain how he ended up in the Chicago River.

"What was the mistake?"

"Think that I should have stayed in my lane," Jules concluded.

"That doesn't make sense to me," Parker said. "I have been all over this city and seen all sorts of things and talked with all sorts of people." Parker fished out his flask. He unscrewed the top and took a sip. "I don't know nobody that will tell you that they were unhappy trying to be great. Mistakes define us, son. Hell, boy, we all are made from our mistakes. When I talk to people, they never tell me that they regretted trying." The saxophonist paused. "They will tell me that they wished that they had more time or that they had tried something that they were're scared of."

"Yeah, but," Jules began.

"The greatest thing any of us possess is hope, son," Parker laughed. "I don't know you from Adam. So, I can't lie to you. I don't know you well enough to lie. So, listen up. Hope is the thing that gets us out of bed every day. We always hope for something better."

Jules listened. He did not say anything for a long time. The pair on the pier quieted. Jules sat on the pier and unlaced his boots. He peeled off his socks. He poured the water out of his boots. Sitting on the pier Jules wrung the water out of his socks as best he could. They were drier but not completely dry by any stretch of the imagination.

Jules climbed back to his feet and took off his leather belt and then his trousers. Parker watched silently. Jules looked at the still dark sky above dressed in his wet boxer briefs. He slowly squeezed his trousers of excess water.

"Now, kid, this ain't that kind of party," Parker scowled. "Don't know how you were raised but I don't undress in front of complete strangers."

"Relax, old man," Jules smiled.

He continued to wring out his pants until most of the water was out of the fabric. He stripped off his shirt and hung it over one of the low pier posts which jutted up maybe four feet from the pier flooring. Jules slipped his still damp trousers back on. He methodically began to wring his shirt of excess water. He knew there was no way to completely dry his clothes, but it was the best solution to a bad situation.

"What was I saying before you started getting all," Parker paused, thinking. "Strip clubbish?"

Jules turned and smiled at the old man and his words. He buttoned his trousers. He was drier but not comfortably dry at all.

"Mistakes," Jules said.

"Naw, I had moved on from that." Parker rubbed at his beard. "So, you done?"

Jules nodded.

"So, what's your plan?"

"I don't know," Jules said. He looked at the saxophonist who was now watching him. "Hey, where are we?"

Parker smiled. The saxophonist furrowed his brows and looked at Jules confused. "You telling me you got amnesia?"

"No, I mean, where are we in Chicago?"

"Well, we are just under North La Salle Street," Parker admitted.

"Damn," Jules breathed. "The last time I remember I think I was near North Franklin Street."

Parker listened. "Yeah, that is a bit of a ways away." The saxophonist calculated. He studied Jules in the darkness. "You sure you're okay?"

Jules nodded and looked down the river in the direction he had come.

Parker smiled. He smiled not because he was happy or amused. He smiled because as Jules looked down the river, back toward Franklin Street, for an instant he wondered if Jules had the backbone to fight whoever or whatever had tossed him in the river.

"Was she worth it," Parker asked for the third time.

"Hell, man, I just got thrown in the Chicago River," Jules said louder than he wanted, and Parker recoiled at the deep bass of Jules' voice. "If she ain't worth that then I don't know no one that is."

Parker nodded.

"But," Jules said only to stop himself.

"But you ain't sure that the fight for her is worth the fight you have to fight?"

Jules ran a hand over his short-cropped hair feeling the water still clinging to him. He was drier but still moist.

"Nothing worth anything is free, Jules," Parker pointed out.

"Yeah, huh," Jules agreed.

The two black men sat on the pier and listened to the city sounds.

Jules listened to the sound of cars over his head. There were always cars going north and south and east and west in the city. That was the one constant of Chicago for Jules. Unlike other bigger cities Chicagoans were 24-hour people. The city slept but not all the residents.

Sometimes, Jules' thought, there had to be moments when there were no people on the streets. But he was unaware of those times. Even in the thick of winter when the wind chill was deadly there were cars moving up and down the streets in Chicago.

Jules looked up and in the lightening sky overhead and knew in a few hours there would be hundreds, then thousands of cars moving on the streets that Saturday morning. There were always cars whizzing by anytime Jules was outside.

Lower Wacker Drive was just above their heads and suddenly a million miles away, Jules' thought. If only he had not listened to Max. If he had just gone home and done what he had done every other Friday night.

"So, how did you end up here?"

Jules took a deep breath. He tried to think of a way to answer the saxophonist. It was a strange and twisting story which had happened just a few hours ago.

"What time is it?"

"Do I look like someone that keeps up with time, kid?"

Jules nodded. It was late or early depending on your perspective. He was not extremely tired but knew that the day had concluded, and a new day was beginning.

Jules decided to tell the saxophonist the whole story from the beginning. Maybe just to get it straight in his own head. Anyway, the whole incident had him full of adrenaline, so he felt compelled to talk. Jules certainly wasn't about to go to sleep.

"What they call you?"

"Parker," the old man said.

"Okay, Parker. If you ain't going nowhere right now, I'll tell you the whole story from the start."

"I wasn't planning on going anywhere," Parker said, with a wry smile. "Go ahead."

Maybe three hours ago, he had been at Cheesecake Factory on Michigan Avenue with Max and a few of his college friends. Max had arranged a dinner with Jules and his friends. Max explained he felt Jules was a little overworked in the throes of trying to cheer up Jules. Max, blue eyed and handsome had all the typical features of a blonde surfer living in Chicago. He was lean, bright and empathetic. Dressed in a maroon high collared slim fit dress shirt with print designed cuffs and designer jeans Max looked like he was still in high school.

At the dinner were Phil, Byron and Rodney. Phil was this round headed tough who liked to wear denim when not working for the city. He was a jowly mustached friendly sort of manager of a department in CDOT. He had gotten the job through a friend of his alderman father. It was a cushy job. That night Phil was wearing his signature denim button up long sleeve shirt and denim jeans.

Byron worked for CTA and was in the tech department and was involved in the retrofit of the first of seven rail improvements. Byron had tried his hand at bodybuilding and gone as far as amateur elites but did not like live competitions. Byron liked going to the gym, and whenever he could, looking for an opportunity to show off his thick biceps. So, that night he was wearing a short-sleeved polo shirt. He was a gym rat and concentrated on everything above the waist and ended up looking like an upside triangle with chicken legs.

Rodney, the round-faced son of David Ford, had the best job of them all, in Jules' eyes. He worked for the Chicago Bulls as an outreach coordinator. His father was somehow connected with the Bulls and got his son a job once he got out of college. He was wearing a Chicago Bulls long sleeve shirt and designer blue jeans.

Of the five Jules was the only melanin rich member of the dinner party. They had a light dinner and talked for an hour before Phil, who had married his college sweetheart, had to head home.

"Jules, you have to come out and see the family. Mary would love to see you and you know the kids love you," Phil smiled as he left. "Stay in touch." Then Phil was gone.

Byron was the second to call it an early night. He was married as well and lived in Lincoln Park. He had married up and into money with one of the Smith family sisters.

Rodney had been all sorts of fun and invited Max and Jules to a Bulls game before leaving. He was engaged to be married to a firecracker named: Patricia and on a very short leash.

Max and Jules after dinner had wandered the streets of Chicago talking.

"Can you believe those losers are so whipped that they cannot stay out later than ten," Max laughed. He added, "It's not even a school night."

"Max, you know you love those losers," Jules said. They were in the front of Jordan's steakhouse after walking to Lake Shore Drive.

"I mean, I do, but they are a little soft," Max smiled.

"What time you heading to Oak Park?"

Max checked his watch. "I got time. Lorraine knows I'm with

you. She would worry if I decided to hang out with anyone else," Max said, after the others had left. Max looked up sheepishly. "So, by eleven."

"You are one of my strangest friends," Jules laughed.

Jules loved Max. He was a great friend. Max loved Jules. There was a mutual admiration for each other.

They walked up Michigan Avenue and Max stopped at the Wrigley Building and smiled.

"What?"

"If you could go anywhere and do anything, what would it be?"

Jules studied Max. Max had a mischievous nature. He also had a dark sense of humor. Those two qualities kept Jules entertained when with Max. Yet, for all the fun there was a sinister side to Max that sometimes-unnerved Jules.

"Well, I don't know," Jules said, thinking.

"You know that right behind you is your favorite place to be on earth, right now," Max smiled mischievously.

"You asked me where I would go?"

"Yeah, you know that you love that building for some reason," Max smiled broadly as he looked at the Tribune building as if he had just won a debate.

"There's something wrong with you Max," Jules said with a shake of his head.

"No, seriously, if you could be anywhere, Jules," Max began. "It would be in the Tribune building. Right? I bet you have dreams of rewiring shit in there."

Jules shook his head. Max could be weird at times but at the same time he was insightful.

"This time Max, you are wrong. The correct answer is sitting somewhere and listening to music," Jules countered.

"I did not know about that," Max said. "Bet you would like to sit and listen to music in that building across the street." He sneered.

Jules shook his head.

"Yeah, I'm not as open a book as you think," Jules laughed a little louder than he intended.

"So, you want to go and check in?"

Jules smirked.

"Okay, let's find you somewhere to sit and listen to music," Max said scanning Michigan Avenue and the Wrigley Building.

Jules just stood and enjoyed Max trying to think on the fly. He had a knack for figuring things out pretty quickly. Jules always found Max's ability to determine the good and bad of things remarkable.

Max turned and looked back toward the west and down onto the lower plaza of the Wrigley Building. At that time of night, the lower plaza was a dark and foreboding space that rested between Michigan Avenue and East Hubbard Street.

"Come on," Max said. Jules followed. The pair walked down the stairs which lead to the lower section of Michigan Avenue. It was not really Michigan Avenue but a quick way to move to the other side of the Wrigley Building.

"You know that if you weren't here, Jules, I don't think I would be as adventurous?"

"What do you mean?"

Max shrugged his shoulders. "I don't know. Chicago can be kind of sketchy at times. But I don't really think anything bad can happen to me when you are around."

Jules smiled and chuckled at the statement.

"No, man, I'm serious," Max confided. "Remember when we were in college and you were doing security for that frat and you had to kick that big guy out?"

"I was doing security, Max," Jules pointed out.

"Yeah, but most everyone else let that guy slide," Max attempted.

Jules screwed up his face recalling the incident Max was talking about. He had been hired to do security at a frat party and there was a strict guest list. Max had been there. Phil had been there. If Jules memory served him correctly everyone was there who had been at the Cheesecake Factory that night. Phil was drunk and useless. Byron was dancing and oblivious. Rodney hooked up with some girl he had met. Max was drinking and enjoying the party.

So, one of the eight security members brought it to Jules' attention there was a troublemaker who was drunk and belligerent in the party. Jules was at the front door dealing with the guest list. Jules had been told to talk to the President of the fraternity if there was any issue. Jules went and found the President and told him there was a drunk who was causing problems. The President told Jules to remove him.

Jules had walked up to the drunk and sized him up and caught him by the wrist and before he could do anything out of hand put him in a wristlock. Max had been following. His security team watched as Jules escorted the drunk out of the party. Max and

Jules' friends witnessed Jules in action as well.

"Man, I told you, I was just doing my job," Jules said.

"You were being a badass, Jules," Max smiled.

"Max, you have a weird idea of how things work," Jules said. "Compared to me."

The two were on the plaza beside the Wrigley Building. They walked across the plaza, Max leading.

"No, Jules, I think it is you, my friend, who has the weird idea of how things work," Max said.

"I just see a problem and try and solve that problem. It doesn't seem that strange to me," Jules said.

"Yeah, that is what is great about you Jules," Max smiled. They went to the rear of the plaza and through a gate and down another flight of stairs. They were suddenly on Dearborn Avenue. Max seemed to know where he was going. So, Jules followed. They crossed the street and suddenly Max stopped. The two stood in front of the House of Blues and Max invited Jules to go inside.

"You know that you don't have to try and cheer me up," Jules said.

"Yeah, I know but I kind of feel responsible for what went down," Max tried to explain.

"What did you forget to warn me that Vivian was a psycho?"

Since their graduation Max had been attempting to find someone for Jules. Every couple of months he would bring someone by or have Jules meet him or come by the house. Trying to find a girlfriend for Jules was his second job, or so it seemed. Jules told him time and time again that he was fine on his own. Yet, Max was driven to help Jules find a partner.

After graduation Max had invited Jules out to his new house and housewarming. Jules had arrived at been introduced to several women, attractive women, that Max had invited to the housewarming to meet Jules.

"Max are you a suburban pimp?"

Max laughed.

Jules loved Max's obsession even though it was usually pretty off the mark.

"Do you have a type?"

Jules was hesitant to answer.

"All right," Max said with a mischievous smile. "Let's look at this differently." Max laughed. "You don't like fat girls? Tall girls? Old girls? Short haired girls," he paused. "I'm close right?"

Jules laughed.

"You don't like flat chested girls," Max said.

Jules raised his hands in surrender. "I don't like how it sounds. I am not looking for what I don't want, Max."

"I know that, but I think everyone has a type and they know what they want in that type."

That was how Max and Jules left it. Max kept trying to help Jules find the least objectionable girl for Jules. It was an experiment for Max, it seemed to Jules to determine the girl that he would like.

The routine was simple. Max came up with some pretense for Jules to meet the prospective girl. Jules would meet the girl and they might talk. That was all that was expected. Jules did not expect anything other than a meeting. There was nothing else implied in the meeting.

In the three years that Max, and Jules had been out of college

Max had introduced Jules to at least a dozen women.

The frequency had been about every three months. The first couple were nothing close to what Jules imagined was his type. There was a couple of months where Max got close.

In the last year, though Max's taste and selection had fallen off.

The last Max had introduced Jules to was named: Vivian. She was a teller at Chase and oval faced with thick eyebrows, green eyes, a nose ring and a nice smile. Vivian had big boobs and liked to wear V-neck blouses to show them off.

Jules recalled the first date he had with the attractive Vivian. They had met at the original Billy Goat Tavern on Rush Street and went to eat pizza at a local spot on Rush. Vivian seemed normal until after eating.

"Jules, let me tell you that I am not about games. I do not believe that we have a lot of time on this planet to figure things out. So, we have to trust in the ancient ones that guide us."

"Ancient ones?"

"Yes, long ago there were these great ancient ones that put all these things that we now call earth, wind, water, sky, light and dark, into place."

Jules listened without judgment.

"I think that you are an open soul," Vivian said.

Jules listened. He did not comment.

That night Vivian and Jules walked around Rush Street. Vivian talked nonstop.

"I am colorblind, Jules. I only see people. I don't trip off the exterior. If you are good people, then I am interested." Vivian paused. "I need to tell you that it may not be visible to the naked eye, but I am mixed. I am two percent African. I am thirty-eight percent Spanish. I am sixty percent Dutch." Vivian added, "I believe in astrology. I also believe in past lives. I am doing some studies on crystals."

Before the end of the date Jules felt that he knew all that there was to know about Vivian.

"No, but I did kind of tell you that she was a good person," Max admitted.

"Max, it ain't your fault that I picked a lunatic who wanted to commune with the ancient ones, whoever that is, and see my soul, but told me she wanted to hurt her father dating me and had no intention of staying with me longer than it took for her daddy to admit he had been wrong about his baby," Jules conceded.

"Yeah, but I feel bad," Max admitted, with a smile.

"Oh, so you took me out to dinner to make you feel better?"

"Well, yeah," Max laughed.

The two friends had known each other since their freshman year at Elmhurst college. Max lived in Oak Park. His father had his own limousine company. They were the most unlikely of friends.

Max and Jules were in front of the House of Blues when a group of people pushed past them and handed Jules a flyer. The flyer was to one of these pop-up parties that Jules had heard about from time to time when in the newsroom fixing computers.

"Let's see that," Max smiled. He skimmed the flyer and looked at Jules. "This looks just like what the doctor ordered."

"No, Max," Jules begged.

"Look, man, as your guilt-ridden friend, who happens to be white, me going to this Club Infused is all sorts of bad, if I go alone.

But, if I take my friend," Max lifted the flyer higher. "I can feel better about myself trying to get my friend out of his rut. I might even feel good enough to let this whole thing between you and Vivian go."

Jules laughed. "Again, I'm the one that is supposed to be feeling bad and you are supposed to be cheering *me* up."

"Sometimes, Jules, you eat the bear and sometimes that bear eats you," Max laughed and suddenly the two were headed to Lower Wacker Drive.

They had stood in line for nearly half an hour and just when Jules was ready to leave, they were allowed to pay twenty dollars to enter the club for a night of dancing with three DJs that were world renowned.

Of course, one hour later Max was gone. He had to catch the last train heading back to the suburbs. Jules had thought to leave as well. The music was too loud. The drinks were watered down. There was a lot of attitude. But instead of leaving with Max he lingered. It was Friday night and there was nothing to do once he went home.

If he went home, he would sit on the couch and watch Netflix or YouTube for a couple of hours and fall asleep. Big night. Being out and about, thanks to Max, gave Jules options. He was suddenly around people. He was listening to horrible music and paying for overpriced cranberry juice and thinking he would leave in an hour.

Then a few minutes from midnight a woman, no, a goddess, walked into the club. The moment Jules had seen the statuesque caramel skinned beauty things slowed, the music fell away and he felt himself falling toward the tall beauty with the almond shaped eyes, straight nose and full lips. She moved like a dancer with a curly Mohawk and braids as she entered Club Infused dressed in a striking white spaghetti strapped mini dress. For Jules, she was the latest Chicago celebrity he had to meet.

Beside her was the thug leader Jules recognized as someone who spent a lot of time perfecting his mean mug and scowl. He was the leader of the ones who stomped into the club behind him and expected everyone to stop what they were doing to acknowledge them. By the mean mugger was the wild-eyed second, Jules deduced. The second, wearing baggy jeans, Timberlands, and an oversized designer hoody had to be the shooter of the crew or the danger boy. Jules studied them just long enough to understand the power dynamics.

The woman, the goddess, though was the real question mark. Thugs did not usually move in the same circles as the supermodels and goddesses. Thugs, d-boys, shooters and the like usually had chicken heads and thots but rarely someone as classy as the beauty now stepping into the club.

Though he could not connect the dots between the local thugs and the beauty Jules found his mind moving away from those thoughts and toward the woman who seemed a force of nature in the club as people separated to allow her to walk toward the bar with the thugs.

Jules stuck around a little longer in Club Infused just to appreciate the desirable woman who, at the time, he did not know. He had never really been a dancer. He knew how to dance but he did not go out of his way to dance. It was silly, dancing nowadays,

Jules' thought. Dancing had devolved from recognized dances to just jumping around, pop locking, pole dancing and grinding. Jules thought it was easier to just enjoy the music.

Midnight came and went, and Jules was still in Club Infused listening to music and drinking watered down drinks. An hour of creating scenarios in his head of how he would meet and talk to the stunningly attractive woman and Jules decided to cut bait. He did not imagine he would end up on Lower Wacker Drive in a pop-up club or hoping to say hello to the most beautiful girl in Chicago.

So, maybe ten minutes after midnight, when he decided to leave, Jules decided to detour for a nature break, before heading home. It was that little detour which allowed him to run into the most beautiful girl in Chicago.

Chapter
Three

The beauty was just stepping out of the bathroom as Jules stepped forward and nearly bowled her over. The girl instinctually stuck her arms out to brace herself for the impact of the six-foot tall bruiser who was Jules Semple. Yet, Jules hearing her squeak, like a mouse, had such control of his body he stopped in mid-step and instinctually reached out as the woman looked to be about to fall.

Jules caught the strange woman by the wrists and forearm and stopped her from tipping over. It was pure instinct. He had not even thought of how to do what he did. But in the moment, he found himself braced and holding the exquisite Chicago beauty who had walked into the club minutes before in his strong hands.

"Are you okay?"

Jules lifted her from her halted fall and straightened up himself. People were streaming by. The music of the club was loud and thumping.

"I'm okay. Thank you," the beauty quipped, and Jules found himself lost in her wide smile.

"I didn't mean to run you over," Jules gibed back.

"It was just a near accident," the woman with almond shaped eyes twinkled and Jules wanted to step closer to her. She smelled like warm blueberries and a faint scent of roses. She looked mildly amused.

Up close Jules found every visible inch of her mesmerizing. Her hair had this incredible luster. Every tendril of her trendy curly Mohawk with flat twisted side braids seemed dipped in bees wax or some other oil. The curls Jules had seen on a hundred other women seemed different and distinctive on this woman. She smiled coyly and for an instant her nose crinkled, and Jules found himself hypnotized by the strange woman's simplest gestures. Jules stood and looked long and lovingly at the woman as an art connoisseur must when given a chance to study a brand-new discovery of a new artist. Jules couldn't help but smile.

"Well, thank you again for not running me over," the caramel skinned beauty said preparing to go.

"Wait," Jules said, awkwardly.

The woman stopped and looked amused again.

"My name is Jules. Jules Semple," Jules said. "I would love to see you again. Maybe next time not running you over."

The beauty lowered her eyes. "I'm here with someone," she said.

"But you don't have to be," Jules volleyed. "You could be here with me."

The beauty smirked at Jules' bravado. She shook her head.

"You don't want to get mixed up with me," the beauty said.

"How do you know?" Jules took a step forward and noted that her head was near his heart. "I've made plenty of mistakes and regretted them. Don't know how I could regret getting mixed up with you."

The beauty looked toward the dance floor. Jules looked back toward the dance floor as well. He saw one of the thugs coming toward them through the sea of people.

"Don't let common sense and good decisions spoil something that could be amazing," Jules said boldly.

"Jules, you don't know the people I hang with," the beauty said.

Jules smiled. He could not stop looking at the beautiful woman in front of him. "Tell me your name," Jules begged.

"Bethany. Bethany Sullivan," the beautiful and alluring Bethany Sullivan said and walked away from Jules.

"Pleased to meet you Bethany Sullivan," Jules grinned extending his hand to the smiling beauty. Bethany snickered, awkwardly. She shook Jules' hand and for the second time Jules held her hand. He was frozen in the moment and found himself feeling as if he was on uneven ground.

He wanted to reach out and place a hand against the wall to steady himself. Being this close to Bethany Sullivan was like being too close to blooming lotus blossoms. She was intoxicating.

She snickered again and walked away. Jules turned and watched Bethany walk away only to see her turn around just a few feet away.

"Do you dance?"

"I can."

Bethany looked delighted.

Jules went to the bathroom and when he came out there was a peanut-colored thug waiting. The thug reached out for Jules and Jules swam through the attempt at grabbing him. Jules also patted the peanut boy down in swimming past and noted he was un-armed. The peanut-colored thug took a couple of steps only to stop when Jules turned and stared him down.

"Stay," Jules said, but barely loud enough to hear over the thumping music in the club. He spun on his heels and looked back. The peanut boy remained where Jules had told him to remain.

So, Jules walked back to the bar. The bar was situated close to the lower dancing floor. There were four bartenders positioned so that two bartenders were on either side of the rectangular bar. There were three male bartenders. They were all dressed in white collared shirts and black trousers. Jules noted they also wore white aprons tied around their hips. One was bald with big ears. He had rolled his long sleeves up to show off his sleeve of tattoos on his right arm. The second male bartender was handsome and slightly muscular. He was not as muscular as Jules. The third bar-tender was the sole black male who was tall and distinctive with a tight haircut that was neatly cut. Around his neck was a ball chain with a distinctive medallion that looked a little like an ele-phant with ram horns. He was rectangular faced individual who was easily six foot five inches tall. He was the tallest bartender in the bar.

The sole female was the shortest of all the four bartenders. She was a pie-faced woman with small round-shoulders with a series of stud earrings up her right ear. In her left ear she had two stud earrings. The female bartender leaned over the bar and asked: "What can I get you?"

He ordered a cranberry juice and paid five dollars for the drink. While Jules sipped his overpriced drink, he checked the time and studied Club Infused. Club Infused was a pop-up club and by the very name was a transitory enterprise. Jules studied the floor plan of the club.

There was a double door entry to the defunct pizza parlor. The entire footage of the club was maybe 1,250 square feet. Jules looked from the bar and to the DJ booth. At the time there were three people standing near the DJ booth. The DJ booth was on a slightly higher stage than the floor. There was a smoke machine. There were strobing lights. Club Infused was a money-making machine. There were easily four or five hundred people in the small club.

Jules looked around the bar and did not see anyone he knew. The peanut boy appeared but did not see Jules. Peanut boy appeared and Jules watched as peanut boy weaved in and out of the crowd and finally stopped near the rear of the club where thugs incorporated were gathered.

There were at least six thugs and Bethany with them. The thugs were messing with girls brave enough to be near them, but they seemed to be pestering them more than talking. Bethany was seated on a stool and the leader of thugs r-us was watching her like she might run away.

Jules surveyed the area and noted there were four tables near Bethany and the tables were occupied by young men and women who were drinking and laughing. The closest table was still some distance from Bethany. Jules opted to move counterclockwise around the bar and sit as close to the end of the bar to listen and watch the activities of Bethany from the other side of the club.

Sitting at the furthest end of the bar Jules sipped his cranberry juice.

"What can I get you pal?" The bald bartender with big ears asked studying Jules' drink.

"I'm good," Jules said.

"No, pal, you ain't good. If you are here, you are drinking hard liquor or you are leaving," the bartender chirped leaning forward to show off his sleeve of tattoos on his right arm. For the first time Jules looked as the bald bartender nodded, and a musclebound security snapped to attention and detached from the wall.

Jules smiled contemptuously. He finished his cranberry juice and ordered another.

He gave the bartender a ten and told him to keep the change.

"Thanks, pal," the bartender said.

"Hey, can I ask you a question?"

"Sure, what?"

"Do you know those thugs over there," Jules said not pointing but tipping his head in the direction of Bethany and the five thugs that were around her.

The bartender followed Jules' head movement and his eyes landed on Bethany and the thugs.

"Yeah, I know them. You don't want to mess with them," the bartender explained.

"I don't intend to mess with them," Jules returned slightly annoyed. "I just was curious who they are."

"Well, I don't know them all by name the only ones I know are Diamond and Cole. They are out of Freakyville." With that Jules realized the problem he was facing.

Diamond and Cole and the others were from Freakyville, Rogers Park. Rogers Park was a rough neighborhood just to the north of Chicago. Freakyville were the biggest gang in Rogers Park. Freakyville was mainly d-boys. They controlled certain parts of Rogers Park but not all of Rogers Park. According to Tre they were small time.

Smalltime gangs still battled and popped caps with people they beefed with. Crossing gangs in general was a bad idea. Their solutions were always life and death solutions.

Jules thanked the bald bartender. The bartender moved to serve another customer. Jules knew he had to move cautiously, knowing Bethany was somehow gang related.

The Chicago Tribune computer tech sat at the end of the bar and tried to connect Bethany to the Freakyville crew. Was she eye candy? Was she a local girl? Was she Diamond's high school sweetheart?

The bartender reappeared and busied himself behind the bar. He looked at Jules and smiled. The bartender leaned close to Jules. "You trying to figure out how that hottie got connected with Freakyville?"

Jules did not answer. Sometimes it was better to just listen. So, he looked at the bartender and nodded, saying nothing.

"Well, the way I hear it the girl's mother got sick or something and Diamond pays for her medical care for some reason," the bartender said.

Jules sipped his drink. He watched the Rogers Park crew from a distance. The bartender lingered. Jules listened and tried to mask any emotion on his face.

"Yeah, people ain't all rainbows and sunshine," the bartender said. "They do the damnedest things just to repay people. Some of them are done in the craziest ways."

Jules nodded at the bartender's words.

"Okay, I have to stop you here," the gray-haired saxophonist said.

Jules was standing on the pier and watching the sky lightening overhead. The first streaks of orange, pink and yellow were appearing to their left, over Lake Michigan.

"You facing off with some d-boys for some skirt?"

"It wasn't like that," Jules said. He paused.

"What was it like?" Parker asked. He studied Jules with his world-weary eyes. The saxophonist stroked his beard and studied the boy standing on the pier.

Jules did not respond. Instead, he took a moment before he spoke. "I had this... I don't know special moment between us. A moment. A moment with Bethany was enough to make me rethink things. She was so open and welcoming and unattainable. When she walked away, for the first time in forever, I did not want her to leave. I felt, and I know how this sounds, physical pain as she walked away."

"Physical pain," Park repeated. He looked at Jules skeptically. "You sure when they threw you in the river you didn't hit your head?" The older man scoffed. "You felt physical pain? Yeah, right."

"I don't care if you don't remember how that felt. It felt like she was peeling off a band-aid when she left. Not like cutting off a limb," Jules said, adding, "And that's when things went all catawampus. The Rogers Park boys got involved. I met Diamond and at the same time, I sort of decided if I was going to fight for someone it might as well be for Bethany."

The saxophonist shook his head. "You a fool kid," the old man said sipping from his flask. "I mean that in the nicest way." He chuckled. "A damn fool."

Jules looked over at the scruffy old man dressed in a patchwork of clothes, combat boots, trench coat and his silver flask. He had slipped back on his still moist shirt and was standing on the pier in damp shirt and trousers.

"You ever been in love?"

"Love," Parker said. "Do you mean love or lust?" The old man looked at Jules and smiled. "Do you know the difference?"

"Yes," Jules answered. He continued. "Love is something that stays with you in spite of the differences or distances. Love doesn't keep track of mistakes," Jules said.

"Yeah, love is not found here," the saxophonist grabbed at his groin. "There are a lot of people that try and make you believe that a boner is love. It ain't. Love is a higher goal than the shit that we hear people talking about when they try and sell toothpaste or the latest car."

Jules snorted and nodded.

"The way I see it kid, you bumped into this beauty from Rogers

Park, and she was the brass ring, all of a sudden. You'll get over her. Just give it a couple of days. Ain't no skirt worth a dip in the Chicago River. I don't care how pretty—beautiful—she is."

Jules shook his head.

"I'm not just interested in Bethany because she's beautiful," Jules began.

The saxophonist lifted a hand and Jules quieted. "You can lie to yourself all you want on your time."

"How am I lying?"

"You saying you don't think this...Bethany is beautiful?"

Jules reluctantly nodded his head, yes.

"Then don't lie and act like you some highly evolved individual. We all are attracted to someone. That's nature," Parker said.

"Yeah, but that ain't the only thing," Jules attempted.

"I hope so," the saxophonist smiled, showing off his uneven teeth. Parker looked like he had been eating rocks.

"Of course, I'm attracted to her. If I wasn't, I wouldn't be on this dock talking to you."

"Yeah. Yeah," Parker said, nodding his gray head. "I thought you were going to tell me how you ended up in my river and on my pier."

"I'm getting to the part of the story that got me here."

"Okay, kid, hurry up," the saxophonist said, impatiently. "You done put a crimp in my practice and Bessie ain't the easiest to appease when she is overlooked."

Jules nodded and looked at the gray-haired old man with the scruffy beard and moustache and for an instant he found himself grateful he could explain his feelings to someone and not be judged beyond his words and actions. He imagined telling Max this story and knowing Max would have been enthusiastically supportive despite the inherent risks of a gangland crosstown love affair. He thought Tre and Harold would not have listened to his story once he mentioned Freakyville or Rogers Park. New Breeds and Black Disciples did not give any gang credit except their own. So, there was only the stranger on the pier who played the saxophone to talk to before Jules decided what to do before going back to his apartment.

Chapter
Four

The bald bartender got busy; Jules noted. Jules was thankful for the information. Then again, Jules instantly wondered why the bartender knew so much about the Rogers Park crew. There was another sticking point which did not make sense.

There was Diamond and Bethany. Why didn't the other thugs have girls with them? The absence of women was interesting and unusual. In the simplicity of gangs there were few things which were either interesting or unusual. So, Jules found himself trying to understand what was really going on in the Freakyville crew.

How much control did Diamond wield? Was he able to keep his crew in check even when he was going out? Did he have that firm a grip on the five smalltime hitters in the club. Of course, what begged the question of how powerful was how powerful was Diamond? His crew were d-boys and while he was at Club Infused there were d-boys in Rogers Park slanging and money changing. Jules thought all this and more when he noticed Bethany climb to her feet.

Jules focused on the exchange between Diamond and Bethany. He could not be sure if he read their lips correctly, but it seemed that just typical stuff.

"Where you going?"

"You brought me to the club," Bethany pointed out. "I want to dance."

It was nearly two o'clock in the morning when Bethany broke away from Diamond, the thug who seemed afraid to let her go anywhere alone. Jules had been in the club longer than he had intended when he saw his opportunity appear.

Jules upon seeing Bethany stand went into motion. The quiet technician walked across the front of the bar and the hundreds of dancing couples and tried to make eye contact with Bethany. Bethany was shaking her head and reading Diamond the riot act when Jules reached the side of the bar closest to the lower dance floor.

There were easily a hundred people dancing in front of the DJ booth when Jules arrived at the corner of the bar. She did not seem to see Jules.

Bethany walked to the main floor, passing just ten feet away from Jules. He watched as she walked to the end of the bar.

Bethany stopped and stared for a long moment at the exit and Jules watched, smiling at her. He looked at Bethany because she seemed torn. She looked like she was ready to walk out on Diamond and his Rogers Park thugs, but something held her back.

The bird beaked boy appeared.

Jules waited and listened.

"Diamond told me to tell you that he was sorry," bird beak stated. "He also told me to tell you that he brought you here to have fun and for you to enjoy yourself." Bird beak frowned. He seemed to have something else to tell Bethany.

Bethany folded her arms.

"Oh, yeah, he told me to tell you that he knows that sometimes he can be heavy handed but he don't mean it."

Bethany pouted, annoyed. "Okay, you go back and tell Diamond Martin this." She paused and let him have it full barrel. She spit venom for a full minute. Jules was impressed.

Bird boy stood there and listened and tried to retain everything Bethany was firing at him to deliver to Diamond. The boy with the heart-shaped face looked blankly as Bethany finished her tirade. The bird boy spun on his heels and Bethany reached out and grabbed him before he could leave.

"Don't tell him any of that," Bethany reversed. "Tell him that I just need a few minutes to figure somethings out. Tell him to give me some space for now. That's it. That's all."

"Tell him that you just need a few minutes to figure things out and to give you some space. That's it. That's all," bird beak repeated. "Did I get it all?"

"Yeah," Bethany said and the boy with the hooked nose headed back to Diamond and the others.

Bethany closed her eyes and Jules appeared magically. Jules beamed.

"You don't need to be by yourself," Jules said.

Bethany hesitated.

"You telling me, someone so drop dead beautiful is here with someone they don't want to be with? That's criminal. It must be my lucky day. I mean, if I was your boyfriend, I would never let you be by yourself unless you told me you needed a little space."

Bethany smiled. "I'm not alone,"

"I didn't say alone, beautiful," Jules corrected. "I said by yourself."

Bethany tilted her head, curious.

"You know you could feel lonely in this club right now," Jules explained.

Bethany smirked and narrowed her almond shaped eyes on the tall and thickly built Jules.

"The difference, my dear sweet Bethany, is that we can chose to be alone." Jules Simple paused. "We don't always have control over if we feel lonely."

Bethany stood unmoving.

"I don't like that you look lonely right now," Jules admitted.

"You don't?"

Jules found himself fencing with the incredible long-legged beauty. "No, and if you ever feel lonely, I will make you feel... not so lonely," Jules stumbled.

Bethany smiled at Jules choice of words. "Not so lonely," Bethany nodded, and Jules felt the invisible pull of Bethany on him. He wanted to hug her. He wanted to take her in his arms and just breathe her in and listen to her laugh. Deeper still, Jules just did not want Bethany to leave him at the moment.

"You are kind of funny," Bethany said.

"Well, I know there's a better word," Jules said but he could not for the life of him think of it. He closed his eyes for a moment to think. "*Unlonely*? Is that a word?"

Bethany giggled.

"*Unlonely*?"

Emboldened by Bethany's light laugh Jules smiled. He felt stronger and smarter hearing Bethany's light laugh.

"Yeah," Jules smiled and stood there before the beauty. "Bethany are you ready to make some bad decisions," Jules asked.

Bethany smiled and lowered her head, coquettishly.

"Well?"

"Give me your phone."

Jules fished out his phone and unlocked it.

Bethany tapped a few buttons and handed it back.

Jules looked down and saw the ten digits which lead back to Bethany.

She smiled.

Jules smiled at the ten digits and then back at Bethany.

Bethany spun on her heels and walked back to the bar and to Diamond.

Having got Bethany's phone number and feeling tired Jules decided to leave Club Infused.

He had barely gotten out of the club when two of Diamond Martin's crew roughly pushed him into the dark and into the arms of two others. Cole and Diamond stepped out of the shadows.

Jules had explained how he had gotten tossed in the Chicago River and the saxophonist had shook his head, dejected.

"That's it," Jules said to the saxophonist. "That's my whole story," Jules concluded.

"That's it?"

Jules looked at the saxophonist curiously. "That's it," he repeated. He added, "I'm through."

The saxophonist paused and studied Jules. He smiled and tilted his salt and pepper covered head. "You ever see a fist fight?"

Jules looked at the saxophonist, coolly.

"Of course."

"You know you can always tell who the real fighter in the fight is almost immediately."

"Yeah," Jules said.

"Yeah. The real fighter is the one with the anger in his eyes. He's not angry at the person in front of him. He's angry that the person in front of him is stopping him from the real fight."

"The real fight?"

"Yeah, the real fighter never concerns himself with the fight he's fighting. There's another bigger fight he's preparing for, whatever that is."

Jules didn't respond. He just looked at the man in the tattered hat and trench coat sitting on the broken chair.

"I've been alive for a while, kid. I've seen some things. I've learned some things. The fight is always about survival." Parker said. He looked back behind Jules and toward Wacker Drive. "Do you feel like you're through?" The saxophonist rumbled. "Are you going to let the most beautiful girl in Chicago slip through your fingers?" The saxophonist asked and sipped from his flask as punctuation. He slipped the curved silver thing back into the recesses of his trench coat.

Jules thought over what the strange man was asking. Was Jules going to call Bethany? Was he going to take a chance on the most beautiful girl in Chicago? More importantly, was he willing to offer his heart to Bethany? On the other hand, was he willing to confront Diamond and the Rogers Park crew and whatever that meant? Or was he going to give up and go back to Logan Square and try to forget the last few hours of his life?

"Well, kid," the saxophonist said. "Is it over? Are you through?"

Jules slipped on his socks and then his boots. He laced up his boots. He buttoned his still wet shirt. The last thing he did was thread his belt through the belt loops of his trousers.

"I don't know," Jules admitted. "I just don't know anymore."

"So, what are you going to do," the saxophonist asked.

Jules did not speak for a moment.

"You going to let some musclebound gun toting thug stop you from finding true happiness?" Parker asked. "I mean, that sounds like the most reasonable thing possible."

Jules looked at the saxophonist and shook his head.

"I wish it was that simple. Bethany, in just a few moments, made things in 2-D seem like 3-D, if that makes any sense. We connected and though it was only for a moment I don't want it to end."

"Connected? What the hell does that mean? Is that some mumbo jumbo shit people are saying nowadays?"

"It means that when we talked it wasn't just bullshit. It was real. That moment, those moments that I was with Bethany were more...genuine than all the moments I had with other women in my life. Bethany was real and there was something there that was more important than any of the others before. I suppose that the more I think about it the more I am determined to hold onto that feeling as long as I can."

"Sounds a little bit like you're high, kid," the saxophonist said. "Did they lace something in your drink at the club?"

Jules scoffed. "No. I am sober. I don't get high."

"You don't get high? Wait, what? How in the fuck do you get through this fucked up world?"

Jules did not respond.

"Me, I drink," Parker admitted. "I play Bessie and drink to escape this fucked up nightmare that we are all trapped in."

Jules narrowed his eyes and studied the old man in the tattered clothing.

"You better than me," Parker said. "I spent too much of my life trying to fit in and it nearly broke me. Bessie and Jack are my only friends nowadays." He tapped his trench coat.

Jules closed his eyes to the old man and nodded.

"Don't start feeling sorry for me, kid," Parker growled. "Of the two of us I am in a better position than you."

"How so?"

"I ain't got nobody throwing me in the river. I ain't got nobody threatening to kill me because of some skirt. I just got Bessie, Jack and me."

Jules poked out his lower lip. He reluctantly nodded.

"Answer me this. Did you know who this Diamond character was before going to the club?"

Jules shook his head in response.

"I bet it wouldn't have mattered if he was Mike Tyson's illegitimate son or Genghis Khan. You would have went after her. Huh?"

"Yeah."

"Yeah, I suppose if I was ten or twenty years younger and I ran into some beautiful senorita I might have been tempted to prove my love," Parker said. "Of course, that would have to be some senorita."

Jules snickered. He tried to hide his laughter as the old man studied him.

"When you climbed out of the river earlier, I asked you a simple question and you hemmed and hawed but never really answered," the saxophonist pointed out. "I'll ask you again."

Jules nodded.

"Well, is she worth it?"

"You know, since I have been here, on this pier, with you, I have been trying to figure that out," Jules admitted.

The saxophonist upon hearing Jules' words climbed to his feet and picked up his saxophone. He slowly and painfully began to move off the pier. Jules watched as the old man made his way back toward another patch of darkness.

Jules watched the old man step off the rickety pier and move slowly toward the low and dark building beside the parking lot. Jules, still moist and dressed in his swimming clothes, looked around the crumbling pier and slowly made his way off the pier and followed the saxophonist. The closer Jules got to the old man with the uncombed hair the more Jules thought the man looked slightly familiar.

Once on the parking lot Jules took a few steps and stopped. The sound of crunching gravel caught the old man's attention. He turned and looked at Jules with his big dark eyes. Jules looked at the saxophonist silently.

"How will I know?"

"How will you know *what*?"

"How will I know if she's worth it?"

"When you know your "*Why*" then you'll know your "*How*,"" the old man laughed.

"But how do I figure that out," Jules asked.

"Hell, kid, I suppose that's something inside you that talks to you." He paused holding his saxophone. "It ain't up here that decides," the old man said pointing to his head. "It's got to be in here, but not just here," he said tapping his chest. "The heart will lie. You have to push past just being attracted to someone. That is a trap. They get older. They get fatter. They say something stupid, and the attraction is over. But the real deal love is a combination of the head and the heart." Parker walked slowly and painfully toward the van. "Love, real love, doesn't focus on the outward. Love, real love, sees beneath the skin. It cuts through all the exterior warpaint and sees the heart." Parker stopped at his van. "That's real love."

Jules stood beside the old man and his rattle trap of a van. It looked like it was packed with all sorts of things. Jules imagined the van was a multi-use van.

"That thing run?"

"When they first made it, I believe it ran like a track star. Ten years later it probably ran pretty good. Now, twenty plus years since it was first made it starts up and moves but I would not suggest that it runs anymore. It more or less trots," Parker smiled his uneven smile. "Just like me. I would be hard pressed to run very far or very hard for any amount of time."

Jules walked to the locked gate of the small building which housed the CDOT intricate parts for the Chicago River bridges.

"Hey, pal," Jules called. "You wouldn't happen to have a key?"

"Why you need a key Superman? Hell, you 'bout to topple the Cosa Nostra. Climbing over the fence of a lousy CDOT business has to be child's play for you," the saxophonist chuckled.

The saxophonist did not talk anymore. Jules did not know if the stranger was correct or not. Did it matter? The stranger did not determine Jules' life or next steps. Jules determined his destiny.

Jules hit the fence and climbed over the ten-foot chain-link structure. He dropped down on the other side of the fence and looked back at the van. The stranger was nowhere to be seen.

He made his way to the nearest train station. Realizing where he was Jules thought about the train station and reconsidered taking a train back to Logan Square. As he walked, he got his bearings. He walked east toward the lake and found a set of stairs which led to Michigan Avenue.

On Michigan Avenue, Jules realized he was just a few blocks down from the two iconic buildings on the Magnificent Mile. For the first time that morning Jules felt his first shiver. He turned to the north and walked toward the Cheesecake Factory and Jordan's Steakhouse. He needed to stretch his legs.

Jules knew he was not going to walk all the way back to Logan Square. He crossed the street. He looked up and down Michigan Avenue. It was not six o'clock and the usually busy avenue was deserted.

The sky above was lightening above Jules' head. The sun was

starting to cast stretches of light in the early morning. Jules witnessed the myriad of a dozen shades of gray and smudged black and browns dissipating before his eyes, retreating. In their wake were the thin fingers of oranges, blues, yellows and whites which signal the approach of morning.

There were the early risers out and cleaning in front of stores. Men with water hoses were spraying the sidewalks in front of retail stores. Down the street and toward Logan Square Jules noted there were half a dozen box trucks double parked on either side of the avenue. He imagined the drivers were unpacking and loading in the freshest meats and vegetables and latest fashions or designs for the clamoring crowds which packed the high-end restaurants and fashion hub of Chicago.

Fashion was lost on Jules. He was happy to have a couple of pair of boots, dress shoes and gym shoes. In his closet were seven pair of jeans. He owned two pair of dress pants. He had two suits. The blue suit he bought for interviews. The black suit was for special occasions.

Usually, when he was not working, he wore T-shirts and jeans. All the other clothes were for work. He shook his head, finding himself standing in front of a window display for True Religion. He looked at the display of two male mannequins reaching out to two female mannequins wearing True Religion gear. Behind them in bold letters read: Summer Is Here!

Jules turned away from the display and looked up and down Michigan Avenue. He was tired. A police car slid down Michigan Avenue and Jules froze. He watched the squad car that Saturday morning with two cops scanning the Magnificent Mile. Jules held his breath even though he had done nothing knowing the mere sight of police was always chilling. A simple ID check by CPD could lead to a coroner's call.

As the two police watched Jules silently talking in their patrol car Jules looked away not wanting to appear suspicious. The cop car passed, and Jules exhaled the breath he had instinctually held. He watched as the police car drove toward the south end of the Magnificent Mile and away from Jules.

Jules still moist from his early morning dip hailed a cab. The cab driver was a brown bearded man with a smile on his face. He patiently waited for Jules to climb into the back of his taxi.

"Where to pal?"

Jules told the driver and sat back. The cab pulled away from the curbside and did a U-turn and headed toward the northside of Chicago. The trip from Michigan Avenue to his apartment took a little less than fifteen minutes.

In the taxi Jules tried to think. He slipped out his phone. His phone sat in a waterproof case. He unlocked it and opened the contacts to see if Bethany's contact information was still there. He thumbed through the contacts and stopped when he found the new contact. He smiled.

Jules checked his messages. He also checked the time and was surprised to find that it was a few minutes before six in the morning.

The sky was now cloudless and blue as the morning sun took the sky. There were just two or three clouds in the sky that early in the morning. Jules imagined it would be hot that summer morning.

"We're here," the taxi driver announced, and Jules put his phone away and paid the driver and exited the cab. The cab driver pulled away from the curb and headed toward the main artery of Logan Square and Jules presumed back to downtown Chicago where most fares originated.

He climbed out of the cab and watched as the cab pulled away. Jules looked down the street where his apartment was located and saw a man walking his dog. The man was wearing a Chicago Bears sweatshirt and matching shorts and flip flops. The dog was one of those hybrid dogs Jules was never certain what breeds had been combined to create it. As the man and dog drew near Jules nodded to the man and the man with a goatee and earring nodded back. The hybrid dog sniffed Jules and lingered just long enough for its owner to have to pull him away and continue their morning walk.

Jules smiled at the man and the dog. Jules smiled at the sun. Jules found himself smiling at just about everything. He shook his head. Jules was giddy. He could not stop from smiling. He shook his head again and tried to put his attention on his apartment building to stop his smiling.

The Graystone building sat in the middle of the block and faced the main artery of Logan Square. North Milwaukee Avenue was just three minutes away, Jules' thought. Jules turned away from his apartment to look at the morning from Logan Square. At that hour it seemed a world away. He knew he was in walking distance of Revolutionary Brewing and an even longer walk to the Concord Music Hall, which he had never been to since he moved to Logan Square.

Jules turned back and looked at the building where he rented an apartment and the physical exhaustion seemed to wash over him. He tried to stand tall but for an instant he wavered. Jules knew he was just a short walk and elevator ride from his home, but he hesitated. He took a few deep breaths and tried to regain his waning strength. He had been amped up on adrenalin. Naturally, the adrenalin had been exhausted and now Jules was moving on fumes.

Jules took another deep breath and climbed the short flight of stairs to his apartment's front door. He unlocked the front door and entered the lobby. He let the front door close and lock behind him before walking to the elevator and pushing the up button. The elevator door mechanically slid open, and Jules entered. The elevator compartment was not very big, but Jules did not mind it as it took him to the fourth floor of the four-story building. His apartment sat at the western corner of the building.

He unlocked his door and entered his intimate apartment. On the opposite side of the door was a small table which had a bowl where Jules dropped his keys in. Above the table was a mail rack. IN and OUT were written on the mail rack. There was nothing in either slot.

Jules walked to the red overstuffed couch which was placed against the wall and the matching overstuffed red chair which created a pseudo-L-shaped couch. The highlight of the apartment were the three four paned windows which looked out and over the street below. In the summer it was surprisingly cool in the apartment because the trees on the street canopied the apartment in shade.

On the opposite wall from the couch was Jules' entertainment center. He had a 40" TV monitor which worked as a computer screen and TV simultaneously. Jules did not have cable TV. He instead had the Internet and a host of streaming services.

Unbuttoning his shirt and entering his bedroom Jules peeled off the still moist shirt and wet clothing. He walked past his sleigh style bed and directly into the small bathroom in the rear of his bedroom. The tiny bathroom held a toilet, a wash basin and a claw footed bath and shower. Jules turned on the shower.

Ten minutes later Jules stepped out of the shower cleaner and feeling better than he had moments earlier. He grabbed a towel and wrapped it around his waist after drying his body as best he could. He stopped and looked in the small mirror over the wash basin at his reflection and studied the dark face which looked back at him. He had a cut over his left eye. He also noticed he had a cut on his chin.

He returned to the bathroom and opened the medicine cabinet hidden behind the mirror and found some bandages. He closed the medicine cabinet and applied the superhero bandages over his eye and on his chin. The bigger cut was over his eye.

Jules slipped on a pair of gym shorts and grabbed a cartoon T-shirt which displayed several DC characters and as he left his bedroom, he scooped up his wet boots and walked to the small kitchen. There was a small kitchen table Jules had bought and two chairs near the refrigerator, a sink and a four-burner stove.

Opening the refrigerator Jules pulled out a protein drink and a plum from a bowl of plums in the interior. He raised his right arm and frowned realizing he had to get his watch back. He opened the protein drink and drank. He ate the plum and finished the drink and went back to his bedroom to sleep.

He did not sleep long. He woke at noon and slipped off his shorts and dressed in jeans and basketball sneakers. Jules peeled off his cartoon T-shirt and slipped on a white T-shirt and then re-placed the cartoon T-shirt over the white T-shirt. He found one of his windbreakers and rolled it into a fist sized clip-on item.

Before Jules left the apartment, he saw Max had texted him. He texted Max back and told him he would call him later. Jules then texted Tre and Harold to see if either wanted to have lunch with him. Tre was unavailable. Harold said he would meet him at Rev-olutionary Brewing at one. He grabbed a leather belt from the closet and headed out to have lunch with Harold Waller.

As Jules was leaving his apartment Max texted again.

Jules called Max. The phone rang once.

"What happened last night? Did you find your true love? How long did you stay? Did you try any ecstasy?"

"Max, you need to calm down," Jules said.

"Tell me, details, I am trapped in daddy land and have to live vicariously through you," Max said on speaker phone.

"Not much to tell. I stayed until about two or three, met a girl. Her name is Bethany. She is drop dead gorgeous. Her boyfriend, not a boyfriend, had me thrown in the Chicago River. I have only been home for about six hours and I'm about to go to lunch with one of my old friends."

"What?"

"Max, I can't do this right now. I promise to call you later and tell you every detail. Right now, I'm starving, and I have no patience," Jules said.

Max did not want to get off the phone, but Jules disconnected after promising to call him later with all the details.

When Jules arrived at Revolution Brewery, Harold was already there. Jules nodded at his good friend dressed in black basketball sneakers, baggy blue jeans and a black hoody. On his nose hung a pair of Ray Ban sunglasses. Above the Ray Bans Harold wore a black Chicago Bulls hat.

"What up Aich," Jules said and gave his friend a hand clap and then a hug and chest bump.

"You been here long?"

"Naw, man, just rolled up," Harold grinned. He was a short and shifty type. He was five-foot six-inches tall and seemed always on the alert and ready to fight at the drop of a hat. Harold had a round face which gave everyone the impression of Harold looking younger than he really was. It did not help Harold had round apple cheeks which made him look, when not frowning, like he was about to smile or laugh.

Harold was clean-shaven. He had tried time and time again to grow facial hair but with no success. On the streets people called him: Baby, as a result. Yet only his closest of friends were allowed to call the gangster Baby to his face.

Jules and Harold had grown up together and despite his gangster reputation and affiliation he was a good friend. Jules relied on Harold and Tre to keep him grounded. Thus, after a momentous night, the reason for the lunch call.

The pair sat in the patio and ordered lunch. Jules asked for a salad and chicken burger and string fries. Harold ordered a pub cheeseburger, string fries and a beer.

"So, you know that you my dude and all, but you know we don't do this. So, I can tell you thinking about something serious. So, what gives?" Harold asked as he sipped his small batch beer.

"Love that about you, Baby," Jules said. He took a breath and dived in with all that had happened at Club Infused and everything after, including the dip in Chicago River and the old man and the saxophone, with a friend he had known most of his life.

Harold had listened and laughed and shook his head at Jules' story. He had gotten angry when he heard what Diamond had done. By the end of the story Harold was ready to go to Rogers Park and exact some street justice.

"You called me down here to buck these smalltime Roger Park niggers," Harold asked, leaning across the table. Jules did not speak, thinking. "I'm in. You my dude. I ain't about to let you be disrespected by no smalltime wannabes."

Jules raised his hands, in surrender. He reached out and tried to calm Harold down. The Black Disciple seemed about to scream or foam at the mouth.

"I'm not asking all that," Jules said.

"But you was disrespected, my dude," Harold pointed out.

"Yeah, I get that but there is a bigger question at hand," Jules redirected.

"What's that," Harold asked, tilting his head.

"Should I try to go and see this girl?"

Harold leaned back in the chair and studied Jules for a long moment. He removed his Ray Bans and looked at his friend compassionately. Harold slipped the sunglasses back on his face and puckered his lips as if he was about to spit.

"You know I ain't the one to give advice that I wouldn't take myself," Harold began.

Jules nodded.

"Well, you know what that old wharf rat told you sounds about right to me," Harold said. "I mean, we can dance around this all day but if you think there is something there with this bee—uh, girl, then you owe it to yourself to ride it 'til the wheels fall off." Harold grinned. "But you knew that already." Harold smiled. "You ain't fall off the stupid truck."

Jules laughed at Harold's intelligence.

"So, what? You going on the other side of the Stevenson to handle this," Harold asked.

"Suppose so," Jules confirmed.

"You want some company?"

"Not right now, just going to find Bethany, first."

Harold nodded. Jules paid for lunch. The pair climbed to their feet and were leaving Revolution Brewery when a white girl, maybe twenty, looked up and smiled. The young white girl, nervous and all smiles, walked up to Harold and put her hands up to stop him.

"Can I take a picture with you?"

Harold smiled and looked at Jules. Jules shrugged his shoulders. Harold smiled and nodded.

"Yeah, sure," Harold snickered.

The girl took out her cellphone and took a picture.

Harold and Jules walked away from the girl.

"What was that all about?" Jules asked as they exited Revolution Brewery.

"I don't know man," Harold laughed. "I probably look like some famous black dude she thinks I am or something else," the street gangster grinned. "No biggie to me. They either love us or hate us."

"Yeah, there ain't no in between," Jules agreed.

On the sidewalk the pair paused. Jules was four or five inches taller than the shorter Harold. Jules and Harold were about to depart but Harold lingered. Jules looked at his long-time friend.

"Hell, man, I'll drop you off on the way back to the house," Harold said with a toothpick in his mouth. Harold cut his eyes and Jules agreed even though he had not planned to go to Rogers Park then and there.

"Let me call her," Jules said fishing out his phone.

"Do what you do," Harold advised.

Jules dialed and after three rings Bethany answered.

"Hey, this is Jules, from the club," Jules beamed.

Harold shook his head.

"You want to meet? I'm about to be in Rogers Park and I would love to see you and make sure you are...*unlonely*."

Harold looked at Jules confused. He mouthed: "I don't think that unlonely is a word, my dude."

Jules shook his head in answer to Harold. He listened. "Are you closer to Morse or Clark?"

Harold grinned.

Jules listened. "Okay, I'll be at the Dunkin' Donuts on Morse in ten or fifteen minutes. See you there."

Jules looked delighted. Harold smirked and shook his head. "You know I'm happy for you my dude," Harold grinned. "If any deserves a little happiness and love it's you."

The two walked down the street to the brewery parking lot. Harold walked to his classic 1965 blue Shelby Cobra with roll bar. The two-seater was Harold's prized possession.

Harold climbed into the fully restored and completely original 1965 Shelby Cobra with the .427 hp engine. Jules climbed into the tiny cockpit of the Shelby and immediately buckled up. The Shelby Cobra did not have the conventional lap seatbelts. The Shelby Cobra had race car seatbelts.

"Don't you ever worry about this beast getting stolen," Jules asked.

Harold laughed. "Nobody's that foolish." He walked to the classic muscle car. "You know John Wick?"

Jules nodded.

"Someone crazy enough to look at my Coffy too long and I would go all John Wick 2 but ten times worse."

"You named your car?"

"Yeah, all the memorable cars have names. So, I named my car after that incredible sexy bombshell Pam mother fucking Grier and the character that made her titties a household wet dream."

Harold started the engine and pressed the gas to allow the engine to roar just a little. Jules found himself smiling from ear to ear. The throaty rumble of the engine was like no other sound Jules had heard before. The tremor permeated his skin and rattled his bones. It was as if he was seated on a living and breathing animal full of unbridled power.

"Ladies and gentlemen," Harold said putting the Shelby into gear and slowly edging the classic muscle car out of the parking lot like he was a little old lady from Pasadena. "Make sure you keep your hands and feet in the machine at all times. Any time I floor Coffy I think of Steve McQueen and how this bitch would have eaten up his Mustang in Bullitt. Here we go," Harold laughed and floored the Shelby and the car fishtailed out of the parking lot and into the street. Harold double clutched and the nose of the Shelby straightened and dove toward the corner.

A couple of hipsters wearing Kangols and golf shorts crossed in front of the Shelby. Harold expertly applied the brakes and Coffy stopped short of the curb. One of the two hipsters looked and did a doubletake seeing the Shelby rumbling at the corner.

"Nice car, man," the hipster declared.

Harold double clutched again and swung the Shelby right and down North Milwaukee Avenue at fifty miles an hour in second gear. The .427 that powered the rare Shelby roared to life and seemed to move on rails as it hurtled down North Milwaukee Avenue at nearly eighty miles per hour in seconds. Twice Harold was caught at a light and Jules knew Harold and his Shelby owned every car made that year or before which dared to try to keep up with the true American muscle car.

"Aich, how did you get this car?"

"I told you this story. My granny was living in Alabama and she knew that I loved this Shelby. I think I had it as a Hot Wheels or something when I was a kid and went on and on about when I was going to get one when I got older. Anyway, she heard that there was one for sell in Huntsville. I found out about the auction and bought it. I had to have it," Harold beamed like a new father, contentedly. He smiled like a kid on Christmas. "It's my baby."

They were on Touhy Avenue and nearing Morse Street. Harold loved the Shelby Cobra more than any other earthly possession. Jules appreciated that about Harold. He knew what he wanted and went out and got it.

Harold slowed, to about fifty, and let the Cobra pull him and Jules down Morse Street. Near the street corner was the Dunkin' Donut shop. He slowed and parked just long enough to allow Jules to climb out of the Cobra.

Jules stood on the curb and Harold did not drive away.

"You cool?" Harold asked.

"Yeah, I'm good," Jules nodded.

"Be careful my dude," Harold warned. "Call if you run into any problems."

"Got you," Jules agreed, and Harold rolled to the corner slow as death. Jules waved and gave Harold the thumbs up. Harold drove on down Morse Street picking up speed leaving Jules in Rogers Park.

Chapter *Five*

The Dunkin' Donuts on Morse Street was busy, but Jules stayed outside and watched as the cars drove by. There was a bus stop at the corner, so Jules went and sat on the bus stop and waited for Bethany to show up. Jules sat on the bus stop and tried to think what he would do when he saw Bethany. Would he hug her? Would he shake her hand? Would he stand around awkwardly.

Jules tried to convince himself that at twenty-five years of age he had a sense of how to react to a woman. Then again, in the two relations he had, neither lasted eight weeks. The first was on fumes after three weeks and ended a week later. That really was not a whole month for the first if Jules was being honest with himself. The second relation with Vivian had nearly lasted a full month before the wheels fell off.

The computer technician tried to think of brighter thoughts. He had seen and talked to Bethany. He had gotten the beauty to give him her phone number. She was interested in him. All that was worth a dip in the Chicago River, Jules figured. He would have been thrown in Lake Michigan if it guaranteed he would get the chance to see Bethany.

Jules looked back and saw Bethany unfolding herself from a car in front of the Dunkin' Donuts. He climbed to his feet. The car was one of those station wagon SUVs which was not a station wagon but not a SUV either. Jules walked toward Bethany who was waving and smiling at the driver. The driver was an upside-down triangle faced woman the color of warm sand with her hair piled atop her head in a soft black puff ball. She had arched eyebrows and big brown eyes. She was smiling from ear to ear as Jules approached.

"Vicky, you can go," Bethany smiled, embarrassed her friend sat in the SUV with a big cheese eating smile plastered on her angular face.

Bethany still had her hair in the curly Mohawk she had worn the night before. She had those almond shaped eyes which held Jules and drew him close, even thirty paces away. She was gorgeous dressed in a Chicago Bulls tank top which highlighted her natural curves. Bethany was wearing comfortable jeans which hugged her round bottom and long legs. On her feet she was wearing some black and anthracite Nike Jordan basketball sneakers with red bottoms. She looked stunning.

Jules smiled broadly reaching Bethany and the SUV.

"Hey," Jules announced as Bethany shook her head and looked in the SUV at her friend, Vicky, who was studying Jules.

"He looking good enough to eat," Vicky said just loud enough for Jules to hear. He grinned not knowing how to take Bethany's friend's comment.

"All right, Vicky, you can go," Bethany said through gritted teeth. "I'll talk with you later." Bethany added, "Remember this is between you and me."

"Girl," Vicky said and let the SUV slide into the street and away from the curb. "Nice to meet you Jules," the driver yelled as she slipped into traffic. Jules looked back and waved awkwardly at the SUV as it receded into the traffic.

Jules turned around and found Bethany looking around skittishly.

"You okay?"

"No," Bethany admitted. "I don't know what I was thinking."

Jules reached out and stopped inches from Bethany. He waited until the tall girl looked and saw his hand. She looked back at Jules.

She smiled mirthlessly.

"Hi, my name is Jules, I was supposed to meet this daring and brilliant girl named Bethany Sullivan I got a chance to talk to last night," Jules began.

Bethany looked at Jules, and a slight smile appeared on her heart shaped face.

"There she is," Jules announced near the Dunkin' Donuts' store entrance. "I found you," Jules said.

"Last night was a mistake," Bethany said jittery.

"We've established that. But I am more than willing to make some more mistakes and errors in judgment with you and to be with you."

Bethany looked back at the sound of loud music coming toward them. She pulled Jules and initially he did not move. She caught herself and spoke. "Can we get off the street?"

Jules looked up and back into the traffic moving down Morse Street. He looked at the cars and noted the cars were nothing special. There were a couple of Hondas, a Suburban, a Cadillac and a bunch of stock cars. He shrugged his shoulders seeing nothing to make him uncomfortable. Jules followed Bethany into the donut shop. She found a seat at an empty table. Jules sat on the opposite side of the table and studied Bethany.

"Why are you smiling?"

"I just... am glad to see you," Jules breathed. "I mean, I actually thought my mind was playing tricks on me."

"Jules, this is not going to work," Bethany began.

"You hungry?"

"Jules, you don't understand how dangerous it is to be here, right now?"

Jules looked around.

"It's just a donut shop," Jules pointed out. "What you worried about your diet?" He nodded and pretended to ignore Bethany's strange behavior. "You pick a place. We can go there."

Bethany puckered her thick lips and for a crazy moment Jules thought the exquisite creature who sat across from him was preparing to kiss him.

"Look, okay, it's nearly two o'clock I have to be back home at six. I'll give you four hours to hang out and if in that four hours you and I don't work then no hard feelings." Bethany declared and looked around anxiously. "Is that fair?"

"Four hours to make a dent in that shell of yours?" Jules smiled confidently. What did he have to lose? "Challenge accepted."

Bethany shook her head. "You don't get it," Bethany began only to stop, suddenly exhausted.

"Oh, I get it, but I ain't going to let it rain on my time with you," Jules said.

Bethany listened and tilted her head just a little to the left, studying Jules.

"You are the most interesting and exciting person I have met in a long time," Jules announced boldly.

Bethany bit her lower lip with Jules' words.

She opened her mouth only to close it without saying anything.

"You know last night was one of the most memorable nights in my life, thanks to you," Jules admitted unabashedly.

Bethany shook her head. She kept looking out the window, waiting for... Jules knew she was waiting for one of the Freakyville boys to show up or a carload of d-boys to show up and try and beat the snot out of Jules if not kill him.

"Can we leave? Let's go to Lincoln Park," Bethany smiled, timidly. "I love going to Lincoln Park on a Saturday," Bethany said looking out of the window of the donut shop.

"I haven't been there in a while," Jules thought out loud.

"Let's go," Bethany begged.

"Okay," Jules said, and Bethany practically dragged Jules out of the donut shop and toward the closest train station, which was just across the street. Jules bought the tickets, and the pair entered the station. Bethany looked back as the familiar silver 733

BMW slid into the strip mall they had just vacated. She walked up the stairs with Jules in hand and into the el station on Morse.

On the train platform Jules stood and tried to relax just a little. Bethany kept looking back and waiting for someone to come storming up the steps and do something. Jules understood her fears but refused to allow Bethany's paranoia, justified as it might be, to spoil his first date with the most beautiful girl in Chicago.

The train arrived and Jules allowed Bethany to climb aboard first, and he followed. She sat and until the train doors closed, she was as tense as a long-tailed cat in a room full of rocking chairs.

Once the train left the station and started moving Bethany seemed to relax, just a little. Jules sat next to Bethany but not up on top of her. He allowed there to be air between them.

"Does the time on the el count against me?" Jules asked.

"What?"

"The four hours you are giving me to make a breakthrough?"

"I'm afraid so," Bethany smiled and for the first time since the donut shop the smile seemed genuine.

"Okay, well, since I am on the clock, you're going to get Jules 2.0. Now, I don't talk that much but based on time constraints I will divulge all the secrets that you would learn in three or four dates on this el ride."

"Sounds interesting," Bethany smiled mischievously.

"Okay, the first thing you need to know is that I do not live with my parents. I live in my own apartment. I have lived on my own since I went to college." Jules paused.

Bethany smiled and seemed ready to laugh.

"What did I say something funny?"

"No, go on," Bethany seemed amused.

"My mom is alive, and she lives in Oak Park. I don't know that much about my dad. When I was old enough to ask questions, he was gone. So, my mom pretty much raised me."

"You close with your mom?"

"Yeah, she raised me," Jules nodded. "I owe her so much, you know?"

Bethany nodded.

"Okay, I am the baby of the family. I have a brother and a sister. My brother lives in Memphis. He is a manager at FedEx. Their hub is there. So, I don't see him too much. He has a wife and two kids. Gerald and Gina are twins. My sister is married and lives in New York. She tried to be a dancer. I've been to a couple of her shows. Pretty proud of her. Think she's going to become a choreographer. Her husband is a music producer or something like that. He took me to a few clubs when I was there. They have a daughter. Her name is Nyella. I'm a three-time uncle. I try to spoil my nieces and nephews. Have a good relationship with both my brother and sister." Jules paused thinking of the biggest pitfalls.

"How often you see your sister?"

"At least twice a year. Of course, it depends on the holidays. We split that up. This year we are going to Memphis for Christmas." He paused. "I will see her Thanksgiving."

Bethany nodded her approval.

"Okay, here come the bombs," Jules warned. Bethany perked up with the mention of something explosive coming.

"What? Have you been arrested?"

Jules snorted as a response. "Nothing like that. Think the closest I came to trouble with the police is them pulling me over because I fit the description of a robber." He paused. "You know how that goes." Jules shook his head. "No, I was going to tell you that," he paused. "I have only had two serious, well pseudo serious, relations in my life. They never lasted more than a month."

"Why?"

"I think I am drama adverse," Jules explained. "I do not react well when others try to make me react. The crazier they get the calmer I get. I used to get triggered as a kid and I learned to control those triggers. The two relations I was in were bad from the start. I got into them for the wrong reasons."

"Tell," Bethany grinned, and her smile spread across her caramel-colored face.

"I got involved with the first girl because I was in college and was about to graduate. All my friends had girlfriends. I didn't even really want a girlfriend. It was just confusing."

Bethany listened.

"It ended with her finding someone who was really interested in her. She didn't really cheat, she just tried to get my attention. I wasn't sure what I wanted. I just knew that I wasn't happy." Jules paused. He studied Bethany. She seemed attentive. He plowed on.

"The second relation was more recent. My friends hooked me up with someone that seemed at first a good fit. She was interesting, I suppose. Then it became a lot of fighting. She wanted my attention. I didn't want hers. It was a mess. She didn't deserve my lack of attention."

"Hmmm," Bethany hummed.

"So, I can see you thinking what about you and me?" Jules reflected.

Bethany made a face but did not argue.

"There is a slight difference between you and everyone else," Jules said. "I am not talking about your drop-dead gorgeousness. I could but I'm not. The difference between the two fails and you are that neither time did I pursue them. I did not search. I did not try. They both came to me. They were attracted to me and not the other way around."

"You attracted to me Jules?" Bethany asked playfully.

Jules chuckled. He tried to control the laughter, but it came unchecked. He shook his head and regained his composure.

"Okay, since I am on a microwave date with the most beautiful girl in Chicago I might as well be honest." Jules looked at Bethany and reached out and his hand to her palm up. Bethany looked down and studied Jules' hand for a second before she placed her small hand in his.

"Yes, I am attracted to you Bethany." He looked down at her hand in his. He smiled. "I have wanted to just touch you, hold your hand since I saw you get out of the car on Morse to make sure that all of this is real." Jules confessed. "This is all so new for me. I thought about you all day and I don't care what the rules of dating say. I wanted to see you, so I called. If I blow it with you, it will only be because I didn't try hard enough and not because I was playing games." Jules looked down and saw Bethany's hand still in his. "I don't want to play games. I don't want drama between us. I just want to make you smile and listen to you laugh and figure out what you dream about and what mysteries are behind those bright eyes. I want to help you get wherever you are going." He stopped, choked up suddenly.

Jules stopped speaking and turned away. He had laid it all out for Bethany to see. He was stripped down to the bone and now, if Bethany liked, she could crush him with one misstep.

Bethany turned Jules back gently around and looked at him so tenderly Jules felt as if he was again on uneven ground. He felt like he was pitching toward Bethany without any control. Jules wanted to swim in those dark almond shaped eyes.

"I like your honesty," Bethany said. She laced her fingers in between Jules' and with her free hand she reached up and placed it on his shoulder. She snuggled close to Jules the remainder of the el train ride.

"Tell me more about you," Bethany asked, and Jules smelled the light blue scents of periwinkle, irises, hydrangea, blue delphiniums and forget-me-nots.

Jules stepped back from the edge he teetered upon just moments before. He looked into those dark and gentle eyes of Bethany and grinned and tried not to gush from the sudden closeness of the most beautiful girl in Chicago. He was frozen in the moment and did not want to breathe too hard or jeopardize its end. Like air he breathed in Bethany.

"Are you okay now?" Bethany asked. Her hand was on his heart. Jules realized she was listening to his beating heart.

"I am," Jules said.

Jules talked and talked and telling Bethany his favorite fruit, football team, basketball team and baseball team. Jules divulged his fear of rats and his on again off again fear of heights.

"I work at the Chicago Tribune," Jules mentioned.

"You a reporter?"

"No, I do computer stuff," Jules said, and Bethany nodded her approval. "I know a few of the reporters though."

"I always wanted to work at a newspaper," Bethany said idly.

"What would you do?"

Bethany shrugged her shoulders. "I don't know, maybe art or fashion." Bethany continued, "I've always liked fashion and wondered why there is no section in the paper for street fashion." Bethany was talking into Jules' chest with her head against his shoulder. "We make the trends. I mean, the designers go to the streets to see what we are doing and then run back to their studios to make their latest designs."

Jules looked at Bethany. She looked up. The dark brown eyes of Bethany looked up and for a moment her smile disappeared.

"What?"

"Nothing," Jules said with a shake of his head. "You are nothing like I expected."

"What does that mean?"

"Nothing." Jules smiled. "I mean, you are surprising. It means you are this beautiful woman and I expected that. Yet, you are not just some empty-headed do-nothing hood rat."

Bethany smiled gently as Jules spoke. She pressed up and away from his shoulder and stared at him for a long moment, silently. Jules looked away and studied the Red Line map which was posted over a handicapped seating.

"You don't know me Jules," Bethany reminded Jules as they exited the train and moved through the station toward the exit. "I might be more hood rat than you are ready to deal with."

"Maybe." Jules nodded. He looked at Bethany. "What little I do know is pretty good, so far," Jules admitted enjoying that Bethany was still holding his hand as they exited the station and descended the stairs to the street above.

"Would you protect me, Jules?" Bethany asked as the pair walked toward Lincoln Park.

"With every breath," Jules admitted.

Bethany fell silent. She looked at Jules and drew closer. She walked on pulling Jules playfully forward with her toward the park and the closest public water fountain.

"Okay, here's a secret. I have never been to a Bulls game," Jules had to admit as he was telling Bethany things that might be an issue if they were to go out again.

"You like the Bulls though?" Bethany asked, suddenly curious. "Right?"

"I love the Bulls," Jules said.

"Do you really?"

"I do. I just missed the whole Jordan era. I played a little basketball in high school, but I was more into football. So, I sort of appreciated all that was going on but sort of missed it at the same time."

"Six rings? How you miss that?"

"I knew it was going on and all," Jules admitted. "I just didn't get all juiced up about it."

"But they won six rings and then MJ took a break and came back and nearly won another ring," Bethany said sounding like a diehard fan. Jules smiled.

They walked along the park walkway. Bethany seemed a different person in Lincoln Park. She seemed free and unencumbered. Whatever had held her down earlier, that heaviness, was gone now, Jules noted. Bethany seemed like a kid, a big, drop-dead gorgeous kid in a grown woman's body.

There was a balloon man and there were several kids around the balloon man. Bethany slowed to weave through the kids. Jules slowed as well and pulled on Bethany, gently to stop her. He waited in line and noticed there were about ten kids behind him. He bought Bethany a balloon which looked like a floating balloon animal.

"Thank you, Jules," Bethany said with a curtsy. Jules could only smile at the free spirit he was near that moment.

A kid ran up and smiled and reached out to Jules.

"Thanks Mister," the dark boy with the balloon animal in his hand and grinned widely, showing he was missing a tooth.

Jules nodded. He turned and saw a man checking Bethany out. Jules shrugged it off and walked a few steps and found Bethany by his side. She was playing with the balloon.

"Can I see your wallet?"

Jules shrugged his shoulders. He pulled out his wallet. He handed Bethany his wallet and seemed unconcerned.

She opened it up and studied it and then looked at Jules. Jules was looking at the kids running around with the balloon animals. He looked back and saw Bethany looking at him.

"What?"

"You are pretty sure of yourself," Bethany said.

"No, not really," Jules said. "I didn't peg you as a pickpocket and if you were, I figured I could chase you down."

"Chase me down?" Bethany laughed. She smiled rebelliously. "I got jets," Bethany said pointing to her long legs.

Jules laughed. "Jets? Okay," Jules said.

Bethany and Jules continued deeper into the park. Bethany tugged the floating balloon animal along with her. Jules could not help but smile at Bethany. There were groups of people seated on the rolling green of the acres of manicured grass. Various vendors walked up and down the park pathways selling all manner of goods.

"You hungry?"

Bethany did not object.

Jules walked to a hotdog stand and bought two hotdogs. He handed Bethany a hotdog and Bethany for half a moment seemed unsure what to do with her balloon. Jules took the balloon and tied the string gently around Bethany's left wrist.

"Thank you," Bethany stated.

"No, thank you," Jules beamed and let Bethany accessorize the Chicago staple.

Jules, a hotdog connoisseur, put every topping that the stand had available on his foot-long hotdog. Bethany and Jules found a bench and sat to eat their hotdogs.

Bethany was trying to be dainty and demure when Jules sat down and nodded to her.

"Bon Appetit," Jules stated and devoured his hotdog. It was ugly and comical.

"You are a mess," Bethany laughed.

"Mess or not I'm hungry. You can play but I don't play about my food," Jules said in between bites.

The computer technician went back to inhaling his hotdog. At the end he had mustard on his nose and cheek. Relish fell off his hotdog. There were a few stray chopped onions on his jeans when he looked up and snickered and wiped his face with his paper napkins, he had taken from the hotdog stand.

Bethany had mustard on her chin. Chopped onions had fallen in between her small feet. She was half done when Jules finished his hotdog and slowly sipped at his can of cold iced tea.

"You are a surprise Jules Semple," Bethany declared.

"How, so?"

"You are this big bruiser of a guy that doesn't seem to fear anything," Bethany started only to stop. "You just seem to be more than that." Bethany looked back from where they had just walked and in the distance, there were kids with balloons.

"Ah, today is a day for unexpected discoveries," Jules chuckled. Jules reached across to Bethany and wiped her chin clean of mustard with a paper napkin.

"You had some mustard on your," Jules tried awkwardly. He looked away embarrassed. He sat and watched Bethany eat out of the corner of his eye.

"So, what now?"

Jules looked at Bethany curious. "What do you mean?" Jules fished out his phone. He unlocked the phone and noted the pair had been at the park for just about an hour. By his calculations he had another hour before he had to take Bethany back to Rogers Park.

"Well, we could go to the conservatory or walk around or just sit and talk," Jules said. "I am with you and whichever you chose is cool with me."

The pair sat near the Eli Bates fountain. On the field there were a dozen kids kicking a soccer ball. Jules studied them for a second before sitting beside Bethany.

"Thanks again for the balloon and the hotdog," Bethany began.

Jules nodded.

"Okay, tell me something that would surprise me about you," Bethany said mischievously. "Where do you live?"

"In Logan Square," Jules admitted. "That it?"

"No, tell me something that most people miss with you."

Jules thought of all the things he had told the delightful woman beside him already. He considered and reconsidered divulging too much. Then again, Jules had determined playing games was not something he was going to participate in.

"I think that it might be surprising that I love this city. I mean I know that it is not perfect and that there are a lot of things wrong with it, but I still love it." He paused and cut his eyes toward Bethany. "I grew up on the westside. It was just me and my mom. We struggled. But I had my friends. That was enough to get me through." Jules stopped talking.

Bethany nodded. She seemed to enjoy Jules' secrets.

"I am a pretty good chess player. If you think you can push the pieces, be warned. I take no prisoners," he added, as a matter of fact.

"I always wanted to learn to play chess."

"I can teach you, if you want to learn. It's easy to learn but hard to master."

Bethany smiled.

"I love to swim," Jules pointed out.

"Jules be honest, I heard that Diamond and Cole threw you in the river last night," Bethany said seriously.

"I did get thrown in the river last night," Jules acknowledged.

"Jules I'm so sorry. I wasn't sure how to bring it up. I didn't know. I only found out a couple of hours before meeting you because Vicky, Cole's girlfriend, was talking about it with Cole when she dropped me off."

"If it took me being thrown in the Chicago River to get to spend this day with you then I'll gladly jump in the river every day," Jules declared.

Bethany could only shake her head. "You are unbelievable."

"No. You can believe it," Jules smirked.

Bethany smiled broadly. "Have you ever told anyone all this stuff about you before?"

Jules shrugged his shoulders.

"Hey," someone screamed. "Watch it" were the next words and Jules reached across Bethany and blocked the soccer ball which was headed directly at her. The soccer ball bounced off Jules and back toward the park.

"Sorry about that Mister," a couple of the kids in the park called. Jules nodded.

"You saved me," Bethany laughed.

"No, you put me in the right place," Jules smiled.

The pair sat and talked for another hour. What was interesting and insightful about the hour was that Jules did not talk as much. He allowed the silence to build. Bethany might talk. She told Jules she was the only girl in a family of three boys.

"My brothers were wild. Adam, the oldest was shot in the streets. I was maybe in junior high school at the time. Andre, the middle one, got caught up with drugs and got taken by the streets. He overdosed. I think I was just graduating from high school when that happened. Angel, the youngest, two years older than me, got caught up in gangs in the neighborhood and is in prison for attempted robbery. He's supposed to get out in three years with good behavior."

Jules listened. He did not say anything. He just let Bethany talk.

"So, now, all I got is my mom," Bethany explained. "She's sick and I take care of her." The statuesque woman wearing the Chicago Bulls tank top explained. Bethany fell silent. Jules listened without expression. Bethany narrowed her dark eyes and tried to determine if she had said too much.

Jules pursed his lips. He licked his lips before speaking. He looked at Bethany for a moment before opening his mouth.

"We are a mess," Jules joked. "We're the most unlikely couple," he stated. "I mean here I am not able to hold onto anyone, or more importantly, not finding anyone to hold onto, and you, the most beautiful girl in Chicago, fighting off men that dream of being with you."

"It's not like that," Bethany corrected. "The creeps that talk to me see me and think that I'm a certain way and they think they can talk to me anyway they want. It's a turn off."

Jules nodded. He did not push. It was not his place to push. He understood the presumptions. He also realized he was nothing like the creeps who talked to Bethany any way they wanted.

Instantly, Jules thought of the Freakyville thug leader Diamond Martin. Jules wanted to know about Bethany's relation with Diamond, but secretly did not want to know. Jules wanted to move past the whole Diamond thing but simultaneously he knew Bethany was avoiding talking about Diamond. She seemed to read Jules' mind.

"Diamond has known me ever since we were in middle school. He was just a friend. He saw my mom struggling and started helping out and one thing led to another." Bethany quickly added, "Angel made Diamond promise to look out for me and my mom before he went to prison. The whole Diamond thing is new. We haven't... you know."

"It's not my place," Jules protested.

Jules thought absently, everyone had a past. Everyone made mistakes. He had made many mistakes.

"I mean, you know my history and you know I'm not a newbie. Those two girls could tell you stories," Jules jested.

"Stories?" Bethany smiled and laughed. "More than one story?"

"Well, yeah. They would not be nice stories or complimentary stories since I was not that into either one."

Bethany smiled at Jules' words.

"Anyway, we both want more," Jules added. "That was my point."

Bethany looked at Jules uncertain. Jules smiled and placed a hand on her shoulder.

"Doesn't that sound like every love story you've ever read?" He smiled happily.

"Love story?"

"Yeah, tough guys that fight off a bunch of thugs to take a dip in the Chicago River can want love too. That feeling ain't just reserved for double ex chromosomes."

Bethany smiled. Her smile began as a curling of her lips and the subtle reveal of half a dimple in her right cheek. The broader the smile the deeper the dimple on Bethany's cheek appeared.

"Remember I want what I been missing?" Jules said and felt as if he had said too much.

Bethany reciprocated Jules' elation. She reached out and hugged Jules. Jules finding Bethany close reached out as well and they awkwardly brushed each other's lips.

Bethany was the first to react. She pulled back and looked at Jules for one hard moment still just inches from Jules. Jules studied Bethany just a few inches from him.

"Did you just try and steal a kiss?"

"No," Jules tried to explain but as he did Bethany smiled and leaned forward again. This time Jules was prepared and when their lips touched, he held Bethany by the shoulders and allowed the touch of their lips to intensify. The kiss, now a kiss between them, lingered. Jules did not rush. He breathed in Bethany. He closed his eyes and secretly wished the moment would never end. As the kiss grew and expanded, Jules let Bethany's gravity drift toward him.

Jules held her and the kiss, their first kiss, was akin to the sound of distant thunder. The whole day had led to this moment and when the thunder sounded windows rattled. Somewhere in Chicago someone might have looked up and wondered was that thunder despite the skies being clear. At least, that was how Jules felt.

Bethany parted her mouth and for a moment attempted to explore Jules parted lips. Feeling her tongue dart into his mouth Jules pulled Bethany even closer. The kiss, the initial kiss, lasted longer than Jules could recall. All he remembered was Bethany's head was suddenly in the crook of his elbow. She looked as if she might have fallen asleep, yet her arms were around his neck. When he broke away and opened his eyes he smiled. Bethany looked so comfortable.

Jules sat on the park bench and found himself cataloging every curl of Bethany's curly Mohawk which spilled into her heart-shaped face. Jules grinned at Bethany's lineless face resting in his arms. She had delicate features up close. There was an unnatural symmetry to Bethany. Her eyes were perfect. Her nose sat perfectly in the middle of her caramel face. Her lips, luscious and full were parted and exposing the very hint of her teeth behind.

For a naughty moment Jules' eyes roamed and took in the exquisite form of Bethany Sullivan. Jules took his free hand and brushed one of the tendrils from in front of Bethany's ear.

The pair smiled. Jules grinned and could not stop grinning at Bethany. She, on the other hand, seemed absolutely giddy.

"Suppose, we have to head back," Bethany said.

The pair reluctantly climbed to their feet. Bethany put her hand into Jules giant paw. She leaned on the solidly built man. They stood for a long moment. For Jules the grass seemed greener. The sky bluer.

He looked down at Bethany and just tried to hold the moment for as long as possible.

"Heading back?" Jules asked. Bethany nodded.

The pair reluctantly walked down the street to the el station.

"So, I think I deserve a few questions."

"Shoot," Bethany beamed.

"Well, I really don't know what to ask," Jules admitted. "I kind of thought you would be like me, you know when I did the first half of the microwave first date," Jules tried.

Bethany smiled and bit her bottom lip, which had become one of Jules favorite things Bethany did before talking. She smirked and Jules prepared for Bethany to speak. "See the difference is that earlier I felt one way," Bethany whispered to Jules, edging closer to him.

Jules leaned forward. "So, you feeling different now?"

Bethany smiled broadly. Jules watched as her smile broadened. He felt his own smile etch itself on his chocolate face mimicking the smile of the first girl he had wanted to kiss in a long time.

"I'm definitely feeling different now," Bethany giggled and pressed her body against Jules. Jules sat on the train as it hurtled north and back to Rogers Park and the Morse station. Jules found Bethany's free spirit refreshing. Here was a person, a soul like Jules, who wanted more. He smiled and laughed as Bethany seemed another person compared to the jumpy and nervous person, he had met earlier on Morse Street.

The train was close to Morse Street station.

"Hey, I do have a question," Jules decided.

Bethany perked up when Jules said that. She was just inches from the computer technician.

"Who's watching your mom while you're gone?"

Bethany crinkled her nose and pinched her lips before answering. "It's not like she needs 24/7 assistance. She's ill. But she doesn't need a nurse." Bethany added: "When I'm not there I ask my aunt to watch her."

Jules smiled at the talkative nature of Bethany. His smile broadened.

"What?"

He shook his head.

"Why are you smiling?"

"It ain't against the law, is it?"

Bethany smiled at the question. She pinched her lips and looked at Jules.

"Do you have a nickname?"

"My girls like to call me Bee but not like Queen Bee but like honeybee because I am a sweetie."

Jules smiled and nodded. "You know that I'm on team honeybee."

Bethany giggled and gave Jules a peck on the cheek in response.

"Where do you live in Rogers Park?" Jules added, "I mean, I heard that there are some rough parts of the neighborhood."

"What?"

"I mean is there a good side of Rogers Park?"

"Of course, there is," Bethany said and punched Jules in the arm as the el pulled into the Morse Street station. Jules feigned as if Bethany had hurt him when she punched. They walked down the steps of the train station and were once again in Rogers Park.

Bethany looked around but this time she did not seem anxious or on edge.

"Got you back on time and whatnot," Jules said with a smile. He thoughtfully added, "Should I walk you home?"

Bethany twisted her lips on her caramel face. Jules noticed Bethany had a fine spray of freckles across both cheeks and the bridge of her nose. He smiled realizing there was so much he was not able to take in when looking directly at Bethany. Her beauty was like looking into the sun and trying to see all its brilliant details.

"I don't think so."

"Honeybee," Jules began serious. "I'm going to be all worried about you if you have to walk back to your house alone. I mean, this is Rogers Park," Jules smirked.

Bethany looked at Jules and after a minute agreed he could walk her home.

"It's about ten minutes away," Bethany mentioned.

"No problem," Jules said and tried to get his bearings before walking Bethany home. His plan was to return to Morse Street and either catch a bus or a cab back to Logan Square. He knew Logan Square was about fifteen minutes away by car and twice that by bus.

"Are you coming?"

Jules jogged and caught up with Bethany. When he caught up with her, she laced her fingers between his and walked down Morse Street and back toward downtown.

"So, I was a cheerleader, of course, and I wanted to go to college but with all the craziness happening with my brothers and my mom getting sick I never got the time."

"What's wrong with your mom?"

Bethany hesitated.

"She has mild dementia. She is diabetic. Nothing too bad by itself but the combination makes life a little difficult."

Jules listened and walked closest to the street with Bethany nearest the brick front buildings which gave way to the two-story prairie homes when they turned on Pratt Avenue. On Pratt Avenue the commercial buildings fell away and there were more and more residential homes with the big wraparound porches sprinkled here and there as they moved to the edge of Rogers Park.

They walked down Newgard Avenue and then turned on North Shore Avenue. Jules chuckled at the fact he had wanted to walk Bethany home not knowing he might be forever lost in Rogers Park thanks to the irrepressible Bethany Sullivan.

"Everyone thought I was going to be an actress or do modeling," Bethany told Jules as they walked on the quiet streets of Rogers Park. Bethany walked and without signaling or saying anything there in front of them was a high school. Jules stopped upon seeing the name of the high school.

"You forget to tell me your family has a school named after them?"

Bethany laughed at the joke. "It's just a coincidence," Bethany said. "I learned pretty quickly Roger C. Sullivan is not a relative."

"What was he some crazy white guy who raped and killed people? You know they love to name things after people like that," Jules joked.

"No, nothing like that, I don't think," Bethany. "He was just some wealthy politico that wheeled and *dealed* his way into politics in Chicago."

"You know, if I was Batman or some incredibly rich guy, I would definitely think about getting into politics," Jules said.

"Why?"

"I'm kidding, I couldn't do that I have a conscience." Jules fell silent. "For the longest the jokes were always aimed at lawyers being vampires. Now, it is that politicians are golems."

"What's a golem?"

"A pretend person. Nothing inside."

Bethany laughed at the idea.

"People come up with the craziest ideas," Bethany said.

"Yeah," Jules agreed.

Jules looked at the high school. He slowed and stopped under the name. Bethany smiled, awkwardly.

"But it is kind of crazy to go to a school with your name on it," Jules grinned. "I mean, at the very least, everyone in the family would all have the PE uniforms? Right?"

Bethany shook her head and pulled Jules along.

"Maybe, you have to have stationery?" Jules continued.

Bethany walked Jules just two blocks more and there were apartment houses.

"This is me," Bethany smiled. Jules did not say anything. He liked the quiet moments with Bethany. She turned and reached out her hand. Jules took her hand and followed her to the front door of her home.

Jules studied the horseshoe shaped apartment house which stretched down the block. He liked the green courtyard in the center of the apartment housing. Jules knew the set-up of the housing development. Each house had a front door and a back door which led to the alleyway where there were dumpsters for their garbage. The only downside of the apartment house was the lack of a parking garage. People parked on the streets all the way around the housing complex.

Chapter
Six

B efore I go, can I use the restroom?" Jules asked. He gave Bethany his best puppy dog eyes. He could not imagine making it back to the Morse Street without going to the bathroom.

Bethany unlocked her front door and allowed Jules inside.

"Bethany, is that you?"

Jules entered the quiet apartment. Bethany held onto Jules. She mimed her actions. She raised her pointer finger to her lips. Jules nodded.

"Yes, Ma, it's me. I told you I would be home by six. Remember?"

"Just need to go to the bathroom and I'll be out of your hair."

Bethany smiled. She drew close to Jules and gave him a small kiss.

"I will go and say hello to her while you...do whatever," Bethany confided to Jules.

Jules nodded. He smiled and mouthed: "Where's the bathroom?"

Bethany walked Jules to a non-descript door just off the living room. She opened the door and turned on the light.

Jules mouthed: "Thanks honeybee."

Jules walked into the small bathroom and noted the pink interior. The bathtub, toilet and sink were all pink porcelain. Above the sink was a gold leaf bordered oval mirror. Behind the sink was a small towel bar with a white and yellow bath towel. In the pink tiled interior of Bethany's bathroom Jules relieved himself. He was in the bathroom just a few minutes. Jules chose to dry his hands on his jeans.

He opened the bathroom door and found Bethany waiting.

"Did you wash your hands?"

Jules smiled. He nodded.

"Got to remind some people," Bethany said.

She turned and reached out her hand toward Jules. He caught her hand and followed her into the small kitchen just on the other side of the front door. There was a small window which looked out toward the street where they had walked up earlier. Once in the kitchen, Jules noted the other door which he assumed led to the back of the apartment or the dumpsters. There was a small table with three chairs. In the center of the table were about twenty or thirty envelopes.

"Bee, can you come here?" Her mother called.

Bethany jumped to her feet and then looked back at Jules.

"Just give me a minute."

Bethany padded down the hall and back to the rear of the apartment leaving Jules alone in the kitchen. He sat and studied the envelopes. He scanned a few of the envelopes and curious looked at several which had the same return address.

Bethany was gone maybe five minutes and by the time she had returned Jules had a rough idea of something which might be a bigger issue.

"Sorry about that," Bethany apologized returning to the kitchen.

"You don't have to apologize for caring for your mother," Jules said.

Bethany smiled and lowered her head.

Jules looked at his empty wrist and again reminded himself he had to find his watch.

"You want something to drink before you leave?"

"No, I'm good," Jules smiled. He climbed to his feet and Bethany led him to the front door.

"Thank you," Jules mouthed.

"You're welcome," Bethany replied.

She opened the front door and as Jules stepped to the threshold Bethany kissed and hugged him. He kissed her back and the sparks which had ignited at Lincoln Park reignited in the doorway of Bethany's apartment. He held her and let Bethany melt into his arms. She just seemed to press closer and closer to Jules. Her full lips parted, and she playfully darted her supple tongue against his teeth and then inside of his mouth. Bethany's tongue found Jules' and the two tongues danced within his mouth. His hands held her shoulders at first and then one hand was on the middle of her back and the other in the small of her back. Likewise, Bethany's hands rested on Jules' muscled chest and shoulder.

Bethany stepped into Jules and for the first time the kiss seemed the prelude to something more. Her hand which was on Jules' shoulder slipped downward toward his stomach. Bethany slowed and rubbed and clawed at Jules' oblique muscles.

Jules felt Bethany's free hand move downward from his chest and though he wanted her then and there to give in, he steeled himself to his own desires. He released Bethany and broke their second kiss and stepped outside. Bethany blinked as if waking from a deep sleep.

Jules too took a step back and surveyed the courtyard and the area and the beauty in front of him dressed in the Chicago Bulls tank top and basketball sneakers. She was this force of nature, Jules reckoned. Bethany would swallow him whole and think nothing of it. It was her nature, the technician imagined. He found himself longing for her devouring and fearing it at the same time. All the things he told Bethany earlier came to mind.

He had never pursued someone before. He had always been pursued. That last part froze Jules. Was he capable of loving someone with his whole heart? Was he ready to be vulnerable? Was he ready to be with Bethany?

"Did I do something wrong?"

"No," Jules smiled. "I told you I have never been in a relationship with anyone I wanted to be in a relationship with before." He smiled awkwardly. He looked away. He turned back and looked at Bethany. "It's a little frightening, for me."

Bethany listened stepping out and onto the small three step porch. She smiled and licked at her full lips, hungrily. Jules wondered if he could have gone back into Bethany's home and had his way with the gorgeous woman.

"Don't overthink this, Jules," Bethany said.

"Well, I guess I had it in my head it would be different, in some way. I don't know," Jules struggled. The Tribune computer technician looked toward the sky for something.

"Jules, do you like me?"

"Of course, I like you," Jules said, shocked. "What's not to like?"

"Think you are a little sprung," Bethany said.

"I'm too old to be sprung Bee," Jules said. "I know that spending just a couple of hours with you I have done more and said more than... with anyone... I thought I wanted to be with." Jules paused and narrowed his dark eyes on Bethany. "Maybe, I got my wires crossed." He smiled. He shook his head. "You asked me how I felt. I didn't ask you. My bad." Jules straightened up and tried to get serious in front of the delightful Bethany Sullivan.

Bethany shook her head at Jules silliness.

"Bethany Sullivan, do you like me?"

Bethany smiled and looked at Jules with a devilish side glance.

"Yes, of course I do. Everything is great."

"Good," Jules said with a sigh of relief.

"Well, let's go slow to go fast," Bethany said, and her words seemed to sooth his uncertainty.

"Can we do something tomorrow?"

"Like what?"

"I don't know," Jules smiled gaining confidence. "Maybe go to

Navy Pier or walk on Lakeshore."

"I'd like that," Bethany smiled. She reached out and Jules moved back to Bethany. "Wait, I can't tomorrow. Tomorrow's Sunday. I have to watch my mom."

"No problem," Jules smiled, disappointed. "Monday. We can do lunch or dinner."

Bethany smiled. Jules smiled. Bethany reached out and placed a small hand on Jules' shoulder. He leaned in.

They kissed for the third time and like the two previous kisses there was a shifting of the gravitational poles and resetting of the sun as Bethany fell into Jules' arms and he just held her there. The kiss was as passionate as the first two and as playful. Bethany's tongue fenced with Jules' before. This time Bethany pulled back and looked at Jules for the first time as a transformed and hungry lioness.

"Well, good night," Jules said.

Jules walked to the end of the apartment and waved, and Bethany walked into her apartment. Jules walked and tried to recall the path he had taken to get to Bethany's home. He was near Roger C. Sullivan High School when he heard then saw the familiar BMW 733i turn onto the street he was on. Jules turned down the closest side street and walked away from the BMW as it drove down the street.

Jules being curious walked to the end of the street and around the high school and to the rear of the horseshoe apartment. The silver BMW 733i was parked diagonally across two parking spots and one of the thugs who had roughed Jules up the night before was leaning on the car listening to music. His back was to Jules.

Jules simply walked up and, using the early evening shadows for cover, made his way to the rear of Bethany's apartment unseen by the thug out front.

Jules went to the backdoor of the apartment and listened to the conversation between Bethany and Diamond.

"You know that I care about you, Bee," Diamond said. "But you cannot disrespect me. I cannot allow you to disrespect me," Diamond raised his voice. "I will not accept that from anybody. I've given you time and respected you and your games. Do you need me to become the nigger that everyone fears in Rogers Park?"

There was silence.

"You know for the last few months I have been hands off, right? I'm respecting Angel."

There was another silence. Jules tried to peer through the glazed window but the best he could make of the interior of the kitchen were dark blotches of color as if through an ice cream kaleidoscope.

"I do my boy a favor and this is the thanks I get? You forget you living here for free because of me? Your mom is living here because of me." He paused. "You want me to stop being nice?" Diamond was seated at the kitchen table.

"Why you threatening me and my mother?"

"Why you disrespect me?"

"How I disrespect you?"

"You think I'm stupid?" Diamond paused a long moment before talking. "I run Rogers Park. Nothing goes on without me knowing."

"What's that suppose to mean?"

"That's suppose to mean that we have an arrangement," Diamond said. "I help you and your mama out and you in turn help me out." Diamond paused. "Mutual agreement."

"Diamond, you know that I am grateful for your helping me and my mama, but you don't own me."

"Bitch, that's where you're wrong. I paid for your mama's healthcare for nearly two years. That shit is getting old," he calmed down. "Your mama cost me. I own you, Bee, until you pay off that debt. Nobody rides for free."

There was the sound of scuffling. Jules reached up and tried the backdoor. It was locked. Jules was suddenly enraged. He wanted to do harm to Diamond for threatening Bethany and her mother.

"If I wanted, I could shut this whole thing down and put you and your mama out on the streets. You are living here because of the good heartedness of me."

There was silence in the room.

"So, tell me who you saw today?"

"How you know I saw someone today?"

Jules shook his head. Never admit anything, the technician thought. Bethany was in trouble.

"I told you. I run Rogers Park. Ain't shit that goes on that I don't know about."

Jules listened and connected the dots that Diamond was laying out. Vicky, Bethany's friend who drove her to meet Jules earlier, had spilled the beans.

"He's nobody," Bethany said.

Outside, Jules shook his head. Number one rule in an interrogation is deny everything. If they tell you the sun is up deny it. If they try to lead you somewhere deny it. Never give them more than they ask for. Jules wanted to rush into the kitchen and sweep Bethany out of this snake pit, but he was powerless to do anything then and there. So, he listened.

"Bee, don't I treat you right? Don't I take care of you and your mama? Ain't I a good friend?"

Jules did not hear Bethany speak so he imagined she was just nodding her answers.

"Do you want me to stop being nice?"

"I'm not disrespecting you," Bethany said. She asked, "What, you want me not to talk to anyone?" Bethany's chair slid back. She was standing. Jules could see her silhouette through the glazed kitchen door.

"No, I ain't saying you can't talk to people, baby," Diamond said, his voice honey sweet. "What I'm saying is that you go sneaking around and meeting up with people that I don't know I am going to start to worry about your loyalty. Me, worrying about your loyalty, might make me rethink being nice and paying bills that you cannot afford, for you and your mama."

Bethany was suddenly leaning against the kitchen door with her back to Jules. She did not seem to know Jules was on the other side of the glazed glass.

"Diamond, you don't own me," Bethany said again.

"Keep telling yourself that, Bee," Diamond chuckled, his voice sickly sweet. He climbed to his feet. "Remember that all of this is because of me. If I want to, I could be mean and have you and your dear mama on the streets by the end of the month. If I wanted. Or worse. You under my protection. I snap my fingers and you become a toss-up before the end of the night."

Diamond walked out of the apartment. The kitchen fell silent.

Bethany mule kicked the kitchen door.

Jules jumped away from the door and looked up and saw Bethany's glazed figure recede and disappear from the kitchen. Jules, at the rear of the apartment, looked up and noticed the shadows had deepened, and night was quickly falling. He headed toward the corner he had most recently come from, when avoiding Diamond and his crew.

The air felt thick as Jules stopped in the shadows. Jules reached the front of the high school knowing a storm was coming. The question was if he could make it back to Logan Square before the clouds overhead broke forth and lashed everyone foolish enough to be out in a Midwestern rainstorm. Jules did not imagine that he was going to be one of the unlucky ones.

Jules picked up his pace. He studied the clouds overhead and saw them darkening more than the night sky. If Jules was a betting man, and he was not, he would have given odds he was going to be drenched by the inevitable storm brewing overhead.

He tried to retrace his steps to return to Morse Street. As Jules walked, he fished out his phone and called Max. He had promised to call Max. He did not plan to be on the phone long.

Max answered and fired his volley of questions he had time enough to consider in the time between the last time Jules and he had spoken. Jules walked and could only laugh as he methodically answered every question Max had. He walked Max through the night before.

"How in the hell did you survive the Chicago River?"

Jules just laughed.

"You planning on seeing this girl?"

"If she wants to see me," Jules said. He paused. "I just saw her."

"Get the fuck out of here," Max breathed.

"It's about to rain here, Max," Jules said as he reached Newgard Avenue. "I'll talk to you later."

Jules snaked his way through Rogers Park and back toward Morse Street. As Jules approached Morse Street, he thought he saw the familiar BMW, but it was not Diamond's BMW. Other people drove BMWs, Jules realized.

A block from the Dunkin' Donut shop where he had met Vicky and Bethany, he felt the first drop of rain. The sidewalk then was dry and hot and now welcomed the sprinkling. Jules crossed the street and made his way to the el station. He did not enter. Instead, he stopped and hailed a cab and climbed in. He told the cab driver the address and after a minute the cab was heading to Logan Square.

The cab turned and the rain fell as lightning flashed. There was a loud crack of thunder.

"The summer ain't summer without a little lightning and thunder, you ask me," said the cabby.

Jules sat back in his seat and watched the weather put on an intense deluge that after just ten minutes was gone. The cab drove down North Milwaukee Avenue and turned onto Jules' street. Jules paid the cab driver and climbed out of the cab. The cab driver pulled away from the curb leaving Jules on the street.

He looked down and considered unclipping his windbreaker.

He looked up and into the dark skies and though the storm had ended as quickly as it had begun Jules unclipped and unrolled his windbreaker. He slipped it on. It was made of a thin wind resistant material.

He did not feel like going home immediately. So, he headed back to North Milwaukee Avenue and to Daisies on North Milwaukee Avenue. It was a short walk. There was thunder in the clouds overhead. Rain fell but nothing to complain about.

Inside of Daisies he placed a quick order and waited. The diner was not too crowded. There were easily forty people inside eating. Jules ordered a Spicy Crispy Chicken sandwich, Sweet Potato Fries, and an Iced Rishi Chai Latte. As he paid and left the rain began to intensify.

He paused at the threshold. The rain was not rain but a drizzle. He walked and jogged the few blocks back to his apartment. He crossed the street and to his surprise found Bethany on his apartment's stoop.

Chapter
Seven

The curly Mohawk was the first thing Jules noted. As Bethany looked up with those almond shaped eyes Jules smiled, amused. The rain was starting to fall. Bethany was standing on the stoop showing off her natural curves. Bethany had not changed since the last time Jules had seen her and as he drew near found himself appreciating the jeans which hugged her round bottom. She was wearing the same black and anthracite Nike Jordan basketball sneakers with red bottoms.

"How?"

"I have my ways," Bethany said.

Jules tried to rewind the day with Bethany and was scratching his head, figuratively, as he unlocked the front door of the apartment and allowed Bethany to enter.

The rain fell in sheets as Jules stopped in the lobby and examined Bethany. Behind them the Midwest drencher intensified.

Drenchers are short intense storms which lasted five minutes or hours and then were gone like a bad dream.

Bethany was like a Midwest drencher but more. She was undeniably beautiful. There was a natural elegance and grace to Bethany which did not need incredible amounts of make-up or overly expensive or revealing clothing. Jules just stood holding his dinner from Daisies and watching Bethany digging her toe into the lobby carpet, like an anxious teenager.

"So, what brings you here?"

"I needed some space," Bethany said. "I asked my aunt to come by and watch my mom and headed here."

Jules smiled.

"How did you figure out...," Jules said, trailing off. He shook his head. It did not matter. Bethany was here, in his apartment building, Jules realized, and that was enough. "I don't care. All that matters, right now, is that you're here."

Bethany smiled and it seemed a bit of an effort.

Jules noticed the effort.

"What's wrong?"

Bethany did not say immediately.

"Come on, you came all the way over here, you might as well get the ten-dollar tourist visit," Jules said leading Bethany to the elevator.

"There's a ten-dollar tour?"

"Yeah, I figured you didn't want to view the bathroom or the inside of my refrigerator or cabinets," Jules said as the elevator rose to the fourth floor.

"Yeah, I don't need to see that," Bethany smiled. Jules smiled.

Bethany smiled as well.

They climbed in the small elevator and Jules punched the fourth-floor button. The elevator rose silently to the top of the apartment building. The pair walked to the last apartment at the end of the hallway.

Jules unlocked his door and ushered Bethany into his apartment. Jules dropped his keys in the bowl.

Jules walked into his apartment and offered the red over-stuffed couch to Bethany as he put the takeout bag on the coffee table.

"Welcome to mi casa," Jules said.

He sat in the matching overstuffed red chair which created a pseudo-L-shaped couch.

"So, what gives?" Jules asked.

Bethany climbed up from the overstuffed red couch and walked toward the street side of the apartment. There she stood in front of the three four paned windows which looked over the street below.

"It's still raining," Bethany said. Jules walked to the window and stood beside the statuesque beauty.

The rain was falling steadily. Under the streetlights the rain flashed white for a second and then disappeared to become puddles on the ground.

Jules reached out and touched Bethany's hand. She turned and for a moment looked at Jules. She looked back out of the window and laced her fingers between his.

"It's really quiet here," Bethany said.

Jules nodded. He gently turned her and smiled at her big expressive eyes.

"So, what's going on?"

"I thought you were suppose to take me on a tour?"

"Okay, you get to avoid the question for now, but I'm coming back to it, after the tour."

Jules walked Bethany to the closest room with an open door, his bedroom. He stopped at the threshold.

"That is my bedroom. There's a bed in there, a closet and bathroom," Jules announced.

He looked at Bethany and she smiled.

"You saw the living room already," Jules said pointing to the red overstuffed couch and chair. On the opposite wall from the couch was Jules' forty-inch TV monitor that worked as a computer screen and TV simultaneously.

Jules pointed to the open door on the opposite wall.

"That is the kitchen. There is a refrigerator and stove in there."

"No sink?"

"Yeah, there's a sink and a kitchen table in there," Jules smiled.

"I don't get to see the bedroom or the kitchen?"

"Sorry, as advertised," Jules smiled. "This is the ten-dollar tour."

"It's nice and cozy," Bethany said.

"Yep, that was what I was looking for, something nice and cozy."

Jules ushered Bethany back into the living room and sat on the overstuffed couch.

"You hungry?"

"What do you have?"

"You can have half of my chicken sandwich, if you want," Jules said. He stood up and padded off to the kitchen and returned with a steak knife. "I'll cut it in two."

"You want something to drink?"

"What do you have?"

"Um, water, pineapple juice, orange juice, I think that there might be a Gatorade in there as well."

"What are you drinking?"

"A chai tea latte," Jules said.

"I'll have that," Bethany smiled mischievously.

"Okay, I'll grab a juice," he said, standing and heading toward the kitchen.

Jules stopped at the kitchen doorway and turned around. He pointed to Bethany with a wry smile. "Now, I remember." His smile broadened. "You asked to see my wallet."

Bethany smiled.

"What would have happened if my address on my license wasn't current?"

"I took a chance."

Jules chuckled and turned on his heels. He walked into the kitchen and returned with a glass of pineapple juice.

Bethany was sitting on the couch and holding the remote of the monitor.

Jules sat next to Bethany and slipped the remote out of her hand and removed the chicken sandwich, fries and chai tea latte. He cut the sandwich in two and handed Bethany her half. She smiled and took her half of the sandwich into her hands. He also placed the chai tea latte next to her.

"Thanks," Bethany said.

Bethany picked one of the Sweet Potato fries from the bag of fries.

"Remember I told you I would come back to the question you avoided earlier?" Jules asked.

Bethany cut Jules a side glance.

"Well, what's going on?"

Bethany bit her lower lip. Jules waited.

"You know Diamond? Right? Well, he threatened my mom. He also threatened me."

Jules listened. He had heard the threats when he was outside of Bethany's apartment. He did not interrupt her or tell her he had overheard the exchange between Diamond and Bethany. He listened and ate his Sweet Potato fries and nibbled at his half of his Spicy Chicken sandwich.

Bethany's version of the story was exactly as Jules' recalled. Diamond had driven over with a couple of his boys. Jules figured one of them was in the apartment or on the stoop making sure no one snuck up on Diamond. The other one was the thug Jules saw watching the car.

"He doesn't have to help out, but he does," Bethany said.

Jules listened. He suddenly started connecting dots. Jules did not have the entire picture but the rough outline.

"I was in a bad way when my mom got sick. I think Diamond was asked by my brother to look out for me and my mom before he went to prison. Things got complicated."

Jules nodded. He was finishing off his sandwich as Bethany

turned and looked at Jules with those big brown eyes of hers.

"You must think I'm stupid," Bethany decided.

Jules seemed shocked by the question. He shook his head. He never wanted Bethany to feel less than because of him.

"I don't think you're stupid. That thought never came into my mind. I do think that you were in a bad situation that you could not get out of," Jules said wiping his mouth with a paper napkin from Daisies.

Bethany lowered her head and placed her half-eaten sandwich on the paper bag the food had come in. She allowed her head to fall into her hands.

"You know that when I was a kid my dad wasn't really in my life. For the longest I built up this picture of my dad trying to come back and be a father," Jules began. "My mom didn't say anything when I told her my dad was coming back to us. She never said a word. So, I sort of built up this belief, this dream, he wanted to come back to us."

"Did he ever come back?"

"Naw," Jules said. "He had left us, and he had started his life over somewhere else." Jules chuckled and turned serious. "I say all that to say that not many people do things out of the goodness of their hearts. They have motives. You just have to figure out the motive or the person to figure out their plans."

"Did you want your dad to come back?"

"Well, I was a kid. Of course, I wanted him to come back. That was my motive. I didn't want to believe he was a snake or a dead-beat or that he had abandoned us. I mean, he was my dad."

"He is your dad," Bethany corrected.

"Naw, he was my dad then, when I was dreaming of him being my dad. Now, he's no one." Jules added, "I suppose I had to move on. Couldn't live in that meaningless past."

Jules stopped talking. He played with the division of the fries. He smiled at the pineapple juice in front of him.

"The world is hard. You have to make decisions that aren't always easy. Some people come into your life for a little while. Some people make your life better. It's up to you to figure that out."

Bethany looked at Jules with those expressive eyes and seemed on the verge of tears.

"It's okay, Bee," Jules reassured Bethany. "We all have to learn to deal with hard truths."

Bethany nodded and looked back down at the table with the bits of food on it. She seemed dejected and broken.

Jules reached out and put his hand beneath her jaw and held it like a Faberge jewel encrusted egg. Bethany looked up and straightened up, coming level with Jules.

She leaned in and once again the pair were locked in a passionate embrace. Bethany attempted to bull Jules over, and the bigger man smiled at her feeble attempt. They kissed on the couch and Jules pressed into Bethany as she threw a leg over his and scooted closer to him. Her arms tried to pull Jules closer. Jules kissed Bethany and without thought felt her tongue in his mouth.

For the first time Jules left hand was holding Bethany by the back of the neck as he kissed her. His free hand began at her shoulder and slowly slid from her round shoulder to the top of her breast. Feeling the round flesh beneath the tank top Jules inhaled, surprised and expectant at the natural joys of Bethany's curves.

At the touching of her breast Bethany intensified her kissing and released Jules' neck to squeeze on his tone bicep. She explored his well-defined and muscular chest. Beneath the T-shirt Bethany found and playfully twisted Jules' nipple.

Jules' cupped Bethany's breast in his free hand and discovered her nipple was already erect. He gently twisted the one nipple to the sounds of Bethany's first churring. The sound was similar to the sound of a purring cat.

Jules' hand which had been holding the back of Bethany's neck released her neck and found its way to her other breast. Bethany's moaning increased in volume once Jules' hands held onto and played with her breasts.

Bethany stopped kissing Jules long enough to look from his longing mouth to his chest and then to his jeans. She put her hand palm forward above his navel and without warning slipped her hand into the top of his jeans. Once inside of Jules' jeans Bethany twisted her hand between his belt, jeans and underwear.

Jules' eyes widened as Bethany found his throbbing man parts. Bethany put her hand around his stiff shaft. She gently stroked the warm and throbbing member in Jules' jeans, her hands suddenly awkwardly placed.

"Bethany," Jules breathed.

"Do you want me to stop?"

"Maybe, we should go in the other room?"

"Maybe, eventually," Bethany said impishly. "Can you turn on some music? I'll turn off the lights and we can make love while the rain falls."

The rain fell for two or three hours the first night with Bethany.

Jules remembered because Bethany seemed to be driven by the rain and the thunder and the lighting. They explored each other's depths and been pleased by the suppleness and pliability of their giving partner. Bethany's desire and passion seemed a bottomless pit. Jules' giving seemed endless. He loved Bethany's skin from head to toe and everywhere in between. There was nothing about the Chicago Venus Jules did not fancy.

They moved from the couch to the love chair, so appropriately named that night. For a wicked moment they had climbed out of the love chair and pumped and grinded in front of the three four paned windows which allowed those curious to look up and into the passion pit of Jules Semple.

Bethany was unashamed as Jules pressed and explored her against the window as the rain fell outside. She was this rare gem, Jules' thought, and Bethany was giving herself to him. He held her hand and marveled at the delicate features of her small hand compared to his.

Eventually, they found the bed. A queen-sized sleigh bed dominated the small bedroom. On the opposite side of the bed was the open door and small bathroom with a claw footed bathtub. But they never made it passed the bed. The pair had fallen onto the bed and for what seemed an eternity found ecstasy in each other's pleasure.

Bethany was naked and as beautiful as she was dressed, Jules smiled. Jules could find no defect in the wheaten hued vision wearing a curly Mohawk. She rolled off Jules and he watched as her breasts rose and fell with her breathing.

Chapter *Eight*

Jules lay quiet and exhausted with Bethany snuggled up against him. She placed her head on his chest. Jules knew she was listening to his heart.

"I'm not a toss-up," Bethany declared.

Jules did not respond. He lay there next to Bethany and breathed the delicious Bethany Sullivan in. He turned to Bethany and nodded. He did not speak. He simply listened.

"I don't have *sex* with just anyone," Bethany continued.

"Good," Jules said with a wry smile. "I don't have sex with anyone either. I had sex with you."

"I'm serious."

Jules did not argue. He did not speak. He held his queen in his arms and drew her closer. She did not resist.

Her breathing slowed and Jules knew Bethany was asleep. He smiled, satisfied. Jules was happy. Jules was content. He had the girl, the true goddess of Chicago. With that thought he eventually succumbed to the pull of sleep as well.

Sometime during the night or early morning Jules woke to find Bethany asleep next to him and under the covers. Jules slipped on a pair of shorts and padded out of his bedroom back to the scene of the crime. He walked to the front door and paused.

He and Bethany had done unspeakable things on his over-stuffed couch. They had sullied his red leather love seat. He shook his head of the heady thoughts and tried to concentrate. On the coffee table were the Sweet potato fries Bethany hadn't eaten and her half-eaten Chicken sandwich. The chai tea latte was now mostly water, Jules decided. He looked at his glass and shook his head.

Jules rubbed his face. He was smiling. He was smiling because for the first time in forever he could say he was happy. Happy? It was more than that.

Had Bethany shown Jules what was possible when he just let himself go and given into the desire to be with someone? The twenty-five-year-old closed his eyes and tried to think. For some reason, this moment, in the darkened living room seemed important. He turned and looked in the darkened living room where he had spent endless hours watching videos, playing video games or listening to music and stopped.

Was he in lust? Did he just want to fuck Bethany? No. He had sex with her, but it was not just sex. There was tenderness. There was passion. There was incredible passion. He wanted her to be pleased more than himself. He gave himself to Bethany.

The thought shook Jules. He never considered himself selfish but to a certain extent Jules knew he was holding out for the right person. He did not compromise on certain things.

Bethany had seemed to welcome Jules' lovemaking. There was no awkwardness. There was no rush. There was just incredible passion. There was fiery heat. Yet, in it all it was also gentleness and kindness.

Jules felt himself smiling again. He rubbed his face and turned and walked back to the living room. Jules stopped in the picturesque paned windows. He looked up and at the light, which was streaming through the paned windows, like twelve square boxes reaching out toward Jules. For a long moment Jules just stood there in his bare feet and shorts and the inkling the girl sleeping in his bed that instant was destined to change his life.

He rubbed his eyes and looked up and through the leaves and branches to the stars. The rain had stopped. In its wake the night was clear and crisp. Jules smiled at the stars visible through the canopy. They had been there for centuries, Jules' thought. They would be here long after he was gone.

Jules returned to the bedroom and went to the bathroom and then went back to his living room and put away all the food on the coffee table. He put all the garbage in the trash. After cleaning up the living room Jules returned to his bedroom and Bethany.

"Everything okay?"

"Yeah, just checking to make sure the front door was locked," Jules whispered. It was the first lie by omission he had told Bethany after he had promised never to lie to her.

The two snuggled and before dawn they got a little frisky. Jules was spooning Bethany and she pushed back against him and suddenly, without words or thoughts Bethany had hold of Jules' saluting general. He let her play with his stiffy just long enough to spin her around to face him. They kissed. They hugged and quite normally Bethany slipped his blood engorged man meat inside of her. As she rode him Jules held her hips and tried not to allow her gyrations to push him to the edge too soon.

Bethany rose and fell on Jules' rigid pole before the sun rose. That summer morning the two made love and Jules held on, appreciating the energy of Bethany. He pulled her down and kissed her breasts then her neck and then her lips. Bethany never stopped pistoning atop his hard on. The rise and fall of Bethany's hips against Jules' pulsing hips gave way to Bethany pushing herself back up to easily straddle Jules.

She crossed her arms beneath her breasts as her moment came. Bethany threw her head back and Jules trembled and felt the first spasms of his release. Bethany rode Jules until he went soft inside her.

Bethany rolled off Jules and laid there catching her breath. Jules was spent.

"You like that?"

Jules smiled. He did not speak.

Bethany tickled Jules' rib cage, but he did not flinch.

"Aren't you ticklish?"

"No," Jules croaked. "Not really."

"How come?"

Jules did not reply. He shrugged.

Bethany climbed out of bed and went to the bathroom. She

brought back two hand towels. Bethany gently cleaned up the excess and took the hand towels back to the bathroom.

By eight o'clock Bethany was up and in the bathroom. Jules climbed out of bed and found a pair of boxers and shorts and slipped them on. He padded to the living room. He grabbed the remote and tapped a few buttons and suddenly the apartment was filled with the light sounds of ambient instrumental music. He turned the volume down a little satisfied with the music choice.

Jules walked into his small kitchen and checked to see what he could make for breakfast.

A few minutes later Bethany appeared dressed in her tank top and panties. She was barefooted.

"You hungry?"

Bethany smiled. "You cook Jules?"

"I don't miss a meal," Jules smiled. "Sit down and I will make you a Jules Semple staple. Chicken apple sausage, scrambled eggs, fruit and juice."

Bethany sat at the small kitchen table and watched as Jules busied himself in the kitchen. He seemed to be very comfortable in the kitchen.

"You know what you said about your dad, last night," Bethany began as Jules pulled two plates from the cabinet on the side of the sink. He had two glasses out and filled them with ice cubes. The cooked and steaming chicken apple sausage links were already on the plate surrounded by the melons, grapes, and blueberries forming a semi-circle at the bottom of the plate. He was scrambling the eggs and plating them as Bethany continued.

"I think I understand what you were trying to tell me," Bethany said.

"Pineapple, orange or apple juice are the choices," Jules said, opening the refrigerator and looking inside. "And water."

"Orange juice," Bethany said. She thinned her eyes at Jules who poured two glasses of orange juice and came to sit next to her at the small table.

"Jules, are you listening to me?"

"Completely."

"Well, I just want to thank you for... everything."

Jules smiled, coyly looking back toward the bedroom.

"Not just that," Bethany smiled. "But thank you for that too."

The pair ate.

Bethany broke the silence with a question. "Did you ever want your dad not to be who he was?"

Jules was finishing his meal and studying Bethany in the morning light. The morning light seemed to make her even more attractive. As she looked at him beneath those eyelashes and big brown eyes Jules found himself fascinated by her ageless allure.

"I was a kid, remember? Of course, I wanted him not to be an absentee dad. I wanted things to be normal, but when I got older I just sort of realized what my mom had realized long ago. She told me you cannot make someone love you."

Bethany sipped at her orange juice.

"You said that a lot of people don't do things out of the goodness of their hearts. They have motives."

Jules nodded.

"What's your motive?"

Jules smiled. "Me? I told you. I just want to get to know you. You're this fascinating person I want to get to know. I want to spend as much time with you and learn all I can about you before I become boring and not interesting to you."

"All that you can about me? I don't know if you want to really know all about me, Jules," Bethany said. "There's not a lot more than you see."

"I doubt that."

"I'm serious."

"I would have never pegged you for a fashion editor or a cheerleader." Jules paused. "Well, the cheerleader thing I can see," Jules laughed.

The pair finished their breakfast. Bethany helped clean up the small kitchen. Jules and Bethany returned to the bedroom. Jules dressed and after dressing he and Bethany made their way to the lobby of the apartment.

The morning after the rain made the humidity a little more manageable.

"Do you want me to take you back to Rogers Park?"

"You don't have to," Bethany said.

"I know that," Jules smiled and pulled Bethany close.

She smiled. Jules nuzzled against Bethany.

Bethany giggled. Jules watched Bethany. She hesitated.

"You all right?"

"Yes," Bethany said unconvincingly.

Jules dialed for a car. The pair walked over to North Milwaukee at a leisurely pace, laughing and smiling at the most normal things. They laughed for a full minute watching a mother and daughter dressed in matching sundresses.

The Uber ride met them on North Milwaukee Avenue. The pair climbed in the rear of the Chrysler 300.

The car ride from Logan Square to Bethany's home was a little less than thirty minutes. Jules sat and noted all the landmarks he had used to navigate his way back to Morse Street. What was surprising was the Uber driver had driven an extra block south to parallel the high school and come to Bethany's house from the rear.

The Uber driver parked and let Bethany and Jules out.

"Thanks," Jules said to the driver.

"No problem, pal," the driver said. "If you need a ride back, I can wait."

"No," Jules said. "I think I'll be fine."

Bethany was at her apartment door and entering when the Chrysler 300 pulled away. Jules walked into the courtyard and found the afternoon cooler than he expected. Jules slowly walked to the stoop and entered Bethany's home. Bethany was all smiles as Jules entered.

"You need to meet my mom," Bethany chirped.

"Yeah, sure," Jules said, and the caramel beauty led him to the rear of the two-bedroom apartment and to a small bedroom where a woman who resembled Bethany sat in a chair brushing her hair. There was a flat screen television on a dresser against the wall playing some movie. Jules tried to figure out which movie it was based on the actors but after a few minutes gave up and concentrated on Bethany's mother.

She was dressed in a light blue house coat and green and blue silk pajamas. Bethany announced herself and knocked on the door as she entered the room. The beechwood hued woman with long salt and pepper hair turned as Bethany entered the room. Her hair was loose and curly and fell to her small shoulders. She had high cheekbones and full lips which Bethany had inherited. Her face was a tad bit rounder than Bethany, but Jules could see the family resemblance.

When Bethany introduced Jules to her mother, Jules felt like he was looking into the almond shaped eyes of Bethany twenty years in the future. Bethany's mother was an older but attractive woman who was nearly twice her weight.

Her mother seemed in good spirits. The small room was dominated by the bed and two dressers where Jules assumed, she kept her clothes and unmentionables.

"So, you are taken by my daughter?" Bethany's mother asked.

"Taken? Well, smitten is more like it," Jules joked.

Bethany's mother was suddenly serious. She studied Jules evenly.

"You look like a good person," her mother said. She continued, "Bethany needs good people around her. She allows too many bad influences to pull her in the wrong direction."

"Ma," Bethany whined.

"She is a good girl. She just needs someone to believe in her and encourage her when she starts to doubt herself." Her mother put down her hairbrush. "What's your name?

"Jules," the computer technician smiled.

"Jules, treat my little baby good," Bethany's mother said.

Jules smiled.

"Where is your family from?"

"My mom is from Alabama," Jules said.

"Jules. What is your last name?"

"Semple," Jules said.

Bethany's mother studied Jules.

"Jules Semple. That's a good solid name. Believe in my Bethany, Jules. Encourage her when she starts to doubt."

"I'll do my best," Jules smiled.

"All right Ma," Bethany said. She pushed Jules out of her mother's bedroom.

"Nice to meet you," Jules said as Bethany pulled Jules out of her mother's bedroom.

Once outside of the bedroom Bethany seemed uncomfortable.

"You okay?"

"I'm sorry about that," Bethany apologized.

"You don't have to apologize for your mom. She's fine. I like that she's looking out for you. I think that's nice."

The pair were in the hallway just a few feet from Bethany's mother's bedroom. Bethany was looking toward the floor. Jules lifted her head and smiled.

"It's cool."

The pair headed back to the kitchen. They walked through the small living room and into the kitchen.

"You want something to drink?"

"No, I'm good," Jules said.

"Can you wait right there? I need to change out of this and into something else."

Jules shrugged his shoulders and Bethany started to leave the kitchen. Jules grabbed her hand and pulled her back to him. She smiled. They kissed and hugged.

"How long?"

"Give me ten minutes," Bethany said.

He looked at his right wrist and nodded. He fished out his cellphone and watched as Bethany returned to the rear of the apartment and walked into her bedroom.

Jules sat at the kitchen table and replayed all the things he had heard the day before. Diamond had threatened Bethany and her mother. He had said he was paying Bethany's mother's hospital bills. He paused. Diamond was a thug. He was a run of the mill thug. He wasn't Nino Brown or Felix Mitchell. He was just some off the corner boy who had some clout. Something did not add up.

Jules in the handful of minutes he had before Bethany returned did a little digging. He scanned the apartment and found the letter pile. He skimmed through a thirty or so letters until he came upon some medical bills on the table. He could not make heads or tails out of the bills. Luckily, he did not have to. He knew people who knew a whole lot more than he did. He unlocked his phone. So, Jules took a couple of pictures. He replaced the bills and was waiting when Bethany emerged from her bedroom dressed in a Chicago Bulls sweatshirt, sweatpants and slides. Her hair was clipped in such a way which made her Mohawk suddenly different.

"Bee, what are you doing for the rest of the day?" Jules asked.

"I usually watch my mother on Sundays," Bethany said.

"Well, I guess I'll head back to Logan Square," Jules said. "Can I call you later?"

Bethany smiled. "I'd be mad if you didn't."

Jules tapped his phone and before he could take a step Bethany was hugging him. He hugged her back and without warning they were kissing. He held her and she ran her fingers up and down his back. Bethany's gentle stroking of Jules' back found him excited from her heady perfume. Jules wanted her then. He longed to press against her and hear her moan with delight.

Feeling Jules nature rise against her Bethany slid her hands toward his waist. Their kiss was intimate and Bethany bit playfully at his lip as her tongue explored his mouth and her hand found the bulge in Jules' jeans.

Jules pushed Bethany away. He pushed her away to stop himself from losing control. Bethany smiled naughtily. She was not as innocent as she pretended, Jules realized. He did not dislike that about her. He just had to be careful. She was the type of girl you didn't take home to mother, he smiled. Well, not after the first date.

"What are you thinking?"

"I'm thinking your mom is just down the hall and, in a minute, I'm going to be making some really bad decisions," Jules said, blinking and not wanting to give into his animal feelings.

Bethany smiled.

"We can go to my place, any time," Jules said. "I just don't want to do that here."

"I get that," Bethany said. She stepped forward and reached out for Jules. Jules hugged Bethany and instantly she was fondling his still hard package.

"I got to go," Jules told himself.

"Don't go," Bethany said with a smile.

"I got to," Jules repeated. He headed for the front door. "I'll call you later. Maybe we can have dinner. If not dinner tonight, tomorrow."

"Okay," Bethany said as Jules stepped out of her apartment and into the afternoon.

"Remember you and me are having lunch tomorrow," Jules said.

"I remember."

"I'll call you later, after I get home."

Jules waved goodbye to Bethany and walked to the corner and turned toward Morse. He tapped his cellphone and at the corner turned to see Bethany still standing at the doorway watching him. He waved again.

Jules walked toward Morse thinking. He called Baby first. He left a message with Baby and then called Tre. He didn't reach either. He texted Tre.

Jules looked at the phone and realized it was Sunday before noon. The computer technician tried to think. It was Sunday morning still. It was not twelve o'clock.

Who would be at the Tribune now? There was always someone at the Tribune. It ran 24/7. Dupre or Melvin would have just ended their shifts a couple of hours ago, he figured. Dupre was okay but no one he would trust with a secret.

Melvin was a little better than Dupre. So, Jules' thought. On the weekends there were three eight-hour shifts. According to his calculations the next person he could trust to see something through for him, on a hunch, was Rico. Rico was this Latinx who had graduated from the University of Indiana. He was a smart guy. He lived on the southside.

Rico would be settling into the office and troubleshooting for two or three hours before focusing on his department responsibilities. Jules texted Rico. It was just a fishing expedition.

"Rico how's your day?"

"Good man. You?"

"Good. Can you do me a solid? Can you tell me who's available right now upstairs doing medical investigation?" He added, "Get back to me."

At Newgard Avenue Rico texted Jules.

"Sam and Ray are in the office for a few hours. Both are solid investigators."

"Do me a favor, R, I'm going to send you some things. Get them to whoever you trust. Ask them if they see anything out of the ordinary?"

"Okay."

He opened up the photo file on his phone and downloaded a few pictures to Rico and attached a brief message. Jules emailed a few of the things he had discovered in Bethany's apartment to Rico with the intent of forwarding it to one of the investigative reporters.

Before Jules reached Morse Street his phone rang.

He smiled. It was Rico. The two Face Timed.

"What up Jules?"

"How is life at the Trib?"

"You know," Rico grinned. Then the long faced brown skinned technician got serious. "You okay?"

"Yeah, why," Jules asked.

"This is some weird shit," Rico said.

"Do you think Sam or Ray could investigate?"

Rico paused and looked at Jules on the screen.

"I just need you to get these pictures to Sam or Ray and ask them who is paying for the medical?"

"Yeah, I don't know," Rico hesitated.

"Just ask Sam or Ray to do a little digging. If there's something, then tell me. If there's nothing, then tell me."

"Yeah, okay," Rico said. "Be careful."

On Morse Street and near the Dunkin' Donuts Jules smiled at his luck.

There was the electronic sound of synthesizers and drums and bass thumping from some speakers as Jules walked down the street. He moved unhaltingly toward the peanut boy who the night before had stolen his watch and was now standing on the street next to a white Nissan Rogue.

As Jules drew close, peanut boy turned and his expression went from smug and joking to alarmed and shocked.

Peanut boy was wearing a zip front hoody, a T-shirt, baggy jeans and Nike Jordan basketball sneakers.

"You have something of mine," Jules growled. He reached out and grabbed a handful of the fleeing Freakyville thug.

Feeling Jules' grip peanut boy tried to sucker punch the advancing and unflinching computer technician. Jules seemed prepared and as the punch was fired, he simply flicked it out of the way, like an annoying gnat. In return Jules fired three punches into peanut boy's face and felt him slump in his grip. Jules retrieved his stolen watch from the suddenly slumping boy's wrist and noticed the sleeping thug had a gun in his waistband. He climbed to his feet and turned back to the where the el station was located.

Out of the strip mall rushed two Freakyville thugs. The street was busy, and Jules backed toward the intersection and away from the el station, watching the two thugs checking on peanut boy. One slapped peanut boy awake. The other thug followed Jules.

At the corner, Jules pulled out his cellphone. He dialed Baby first. He then dialed Tre.

Tre answered.

"How long?"

"Give me five," Tre answered.

Jules smiled.

"Take your time," Jules said looking down the street and seeing the two boys walking menacingly toward him.

Chapter *Nine*

Tre and Harold had grown up in the same neighborhood as Jules. Altre Henderson and Harold Waller had been friends for nearly a quarter of a century. They all lived in the same apartment house, just a few doors down from Jules and his mother. All three had grown up together. When they got to be eleven or twelve the street pressures appeared in the form of the Disciples, Black Gangster cliques. Tre had found himself welcomed by the New Breed. Harold had been recruited and found himself one of the street soldiers of the Black Gangster Disciples.

Eventually, when Jules went to college Tre had moved to the Fulton River District and bought a house. Harold had left the apartment complex and moved to Goose Island and secured himself a loft.

Jules noted the two friends and their gang ties when Tre and Harold came rolling down Ashland Avenue in a dark blue Cadillac

Escalade. They did not appear as Disciples. They appeared as friends coming to the aid of another friend.

Tre was driving. Harold, wearing his Ray Bans, rolled down his window dressed in a white athletic T-shirt and stuck his head out.

"You get yourself in trouble?"

Jules smiled. He looked back.

Harold looked back and saw the two thugs walking toward Jules. Harold smiled. The Black Gangster Disciple looked back into the SUV and the blue Escalade pulled to the curb.

Jules stepped to the Escalade. Harold stepped out of the Escalade wearing loose fitting jeans and Nike Jordan basketball sneakers and carrying a blued Uzi.

"You want some of this?" Harold lifted the Uzi into the air and the tight muscles across his shoulders and arms flexed. "You testing me?" Harold lifted the sub-machine gun and the two thugs who had been following Jules ducked and covered and retreated.

Tre, wearing a black Bulls button front jersey, unbuttoned, a white T-shirt, loose fitting jeans, was standing on the door frame of his driver's side watching the two thugs, holding a machine pistol. He had a matching black Bulls fitted baseball cap on his round head. Around his neck was a thick gold chain and Bulls' mascot in gold and diamonds.

"Get in the truck nigger," Tre laughed showing his gold tooth. "Stop scaring folk."

Harold backed toward the SUV. Jules climbed into the Escalade. Harold reached the SUV and he and Tre climbed back into the lush interior of the vehicle.

"We, good?"

"Yeah, we, good," Harold said and closed the Escalade's door as Tre pulled away from the curb.

The Escalade was a big SUV with three rows of seats. It had a gray leather interior. Jules sat in the middle to see Tre and Harold. Harold was the first to slip the Uzi under his seat. Tre drove with the machine pistol on his lap.

There was this trippy, electronic music that seemed a blend of jazz and hip hop but only instrumentals playing endlessly in the SUV. It was one of the greatest soundtracks Jules had ever heard because it was not just rap music or one thing but a combination of several things.

"Reminds me of the old times when we had to save your ass, back in the old neighborhood," Tre smiled cutting a brief look at Jules.

"Yeah, this ain't even as bad as when you decided to go and visit Bryn Mawr," Harold smiled, looking back at Jules. Jules only shook his head.

"We had to go in there hard and shut down things because you didn't believe those stuck-up crackers were that bad."

"Okay," Jules said. He raised his hand in surrender. "Thanks."

"What were you doing in Freakyville anyway?" Tre asked.

"I thought I told you, Tre," Harold laughed. "Jules hooked up with some Rogers Park trim and now he thinks he's Superman, Batman and Aquaman all at once."

Jules did not argue. There was no point. Harold told the story of Jules and Bethany better than he would have. So, he listened. Tre laughed as they drove down Ashland and back to Logan Square.

"Wait, you got thrown in the Chicago River for this girl?"

Jules looked up and found the two gangsters looking at him. They were at a traffic light waiting for the light to change. Jules put his stolen watch back on his wrist.

"Yes," Jules said. He looked to Harold. Harold only smiled.

"You know that we don't lie to each other, my dude?" Harold said.

"You fucking?"

Jules did not answer.

"You sniffing at it?" Tre smiled.

"He paining for it," Harold laughed. "I bet."

"Yeah, that's why he went back over to the spot to keep her thinking of him," Tre laughed. "That don't mean shit, Jules. You got to get her in her skin suit. Then shit goes good." Tre smiled. "Once you get a bitch into her skin suit shit gets awful good, man. Awful good."

Harold laughed. His laugh was more a cackle than a laugh. Tre whistled and laughed.

"They ain't fucking, far as I know," Harold said. "They only got to see each other yesterday." He paused. "Jules ain't no street Casanova."

Jules smiled. He lowered his head and remained quiet.

"Jules ain't a bunch of things," Tre said. "But my baby brother from another mother, watch yourself. Don't let no trim get you caught up in shit you cannot handle."

The Escalade got quiet.

"Hey, you hungry?" Harold asked.

"What you thinking?"

"Jules took me to this brewery on North Milwaukee Avenue. It's close." Harold looked at Jules. "You hungry killer?"

Jules laughed.

"Okay, where we going?"

Harold gave directions. Tre wheeled the SUV like a high-paid chauffeur. The Escalade found North Milwaukee Avenue and the Revolution Brewery.

They parked in the rear parking lot and prepared for a late lunch.

"You eat here?"

"Yesterday, with Jules," Harold said.

"The place cool?"

"It is, we ain't got to be all posted up or nothing," Harold said.

Tre slipped his machine pistol in his waistband and made sure his loose-fitting jersey hid the hand cannon. "You know I think that I'm going to get a holster. I think that will eliminate all this."

"You know you can leave that?" Jules said, knowing the response he would receive.

"Yeah, I know that Jules. But the way I see it I'd rather have it and not need it than need it and not have it."

Harold chuckled. He had a Chicago Cubs baseball jersey with Ernie Banks number and name on it he wore into the brewery. He was not wearing a baseball cap and his neatly trimmed hair was on display with his signature lightning bolt cut into the part on the right side of his head.

"Life on the streets, my dude," Harold said as they were seated on the patio.

As they waited to be served Tre was the first to pull out his cell-phone and make a number of phone calls. Harold was the next to make half a dozen calls.

"Think I want to take Bethany to the museum tomorrow?" Jules told Tre, while Harold was finishing a call.

"What?"

"Three days in a row, my dude?"

"Yeah, you need to pull back. Let her breathe," Tre said.

"Yeah, my dude, don't suffocate your newbie," Harold smiled.

"Naw, all that game playing is out for me," Jules said.

"I know she's your crush and all, my dude, but you need to let her miss you a bit."

"Why?"

"I think that the more they see you the more they start to question if they can do without you," Tre smirked.

"I don't know about that," Harold said. "I think that everyone needs some space, even you, my dude." Harold added, "I mean, if I was always over you might start not to look forward to seeing me. You dig?"

"I do, but I don't know if something so new can get stale?" Jules said.

"No one said that it was stale, Jules," Tre said.

"All I'm saying is that you need to pump the brakes a little and let her want to see you."

"But I ain't interested in playing," Jules began.

"We get it, nigger. You don't want to play games. But ain't that playing games, in a way?"

"How is *that* playing games?"

"You both interested. You both know. You both trying to deal with that newness," Tre said.

"Yeah, that's its own game," Harold said. "It's just a different game, my dude."

"I don't see that."

"You ain't gotta see that," Tre growled.

"Shit is all a game, you ask me," Harold said.

"A game?"

"We're all playing a game," Tre said. "You trying to be the for real, computer technician that ain't into games. That's your game."

"Me, I'm a lost black boy turned gangster," Harold laughed.

"Me, I'm just a product of society turned into a gangster," Tre laughed. "Shit ain't original."

Their food arrived. The three ate and talked.

"You see the problem with pressing a softie is that they start to think you are sprung on them and then they fuck things up."

Harold nodded in agreement. Jules recalled Bethany asking him if he was sprung. The note struck a little close to the bone.

"I don't care what you gangsters think," Jules said as he ate his turkey burger.

"You do," Harold smiled. "You know that we know what we're talking about."

"He definitely cares," Tre said eating his cheeseburger.

"Look at him, he's all in his head, thinking," Tre sneered.

"What you thinking about Jules?"

"I'm thinking about next week," Jules said.

"Next week?"

"You ain't going to give her no room to move? Hardcourt press?" Harold laughed.

"Okay, since you are going all GI Joe," Tre said. "What you thinking?" Tre asked with a shake of his head.

"Maybe going to the museum? Or to the bean?"

Tre made a sour face. Harold smirked.

"Just want to do some things I never did or thought to do with anyone else."

"Museum? Kind of lame, my dude," Harold said.

"Yeah, you met this softie at a club," Tre reminded Jules. "You sure she don't want to go to a club or someplace trendy?" Tre paused. "Why not take her to Jordan's?"

"Everybody likes Jordan's."

"They all go there and hope that Jordan is going to be there or something."

"Man, anytime I am near there I am looking for Jordan," Tre said. "I don't know what I would do if I saw him. I probably pull over and get his autograph or a picture."

Jules did not answer. Tre made a good point. Jules had not even talked to Bethany since he recovered his watch and Tre and Harold bailed him out of trouble on Ashland Avenue.

"I'll call her and see what her day is like and see what she wants to do, if anything, tomorrow," Jules said to Tre and Harold.

"Better plan is to give her some choices," Tre said. "Softies like hardheads who have a plan." Tre added, "Tell her what you want to do."

"Yeah, I agree with Tre on that one, my dude," Harold chuckled. "Most of my fails came from asking them what they wanted to do.

We lead. They follow."

Jules thought about what his friends said.

Harold and Tre climbed to their feet. Lunch was suddenly over. Tre pulled out a hundred-dollar bill and dropped it on the table. Harold, not to be outdone, pulled a hundred out of his pocket and dropped it on the table. Jules did not say a word. The pair had left the server a sixty-dollar tip.

"Thank you, my brothers, from other mothers," Jules said on the sidewalk, giving each gangster a hug and pat on the back.

"Be frosty, my dude," Harold said.

"Stay out of trouble, Jules," Tre advised. "We ain't always going to be around to be your bodyguards."

"Bull," Jules laughed. "You is always going to be around because you my boys. And I am always your boy."

Jules walked to his apartment and as he did, he called up Max, again.

He talked with his good friend for a few more minutes and then hung up.

After calling Max and before he made it to the Graystone he called Bethany. He checked the time and was surprised to find that it was nearly five o'clock. Hanging with Tre and Harold was timeless. It was Sunday and Jules had to prepare for work the following day. He had a few things to do around his apartment.

"Hey, Bee, it's me, Jules," he said, almost stuttering. Bethany was still a delicate and fragile thing.

"Well, I'm just getting home. Ran into some friends and we had a late lunch. They just left. We went to the brewery just down the street." He paused and listened. "How is your mom?" He listened to Bethany. "I was calling to figure out what we are doing tomorrow? I know you are with your mom tonight and I just wanted to see if you want to do something at lunch or after work. I mean I will be off at six." He listened to Bethany. "Well, there are all sorts of things we can do. I mean, it's Chicago. We can go to a museum. We can walk LSD. We could go to the bean. Or Buckingham fountain. Iconic stuff. Touristy stuff. We could walk on State Street mall." Jules paused. "I just would like to see you."

There was a pause.

Chapter Ten

The Chicago Tribune office was located on Michigan Avenue. 435 Michigan Avenue to be exact. The Tribune Tower rose thirty-four stories into the air in a neo gothic architecture created by Raymond Hood and John Mead Howells. Jules loved he knew so much about the Tribune Tower. Every time he came out to the lobby there was usually a tour going on and the guide would tell the gathered the lobby of the Tribune Tower had two distinct features. There was a giant relief map made up of shredded money. Jules would look with the visitors at the second unique element of the Tribune lobby which was also called the Hall of Inscriptions. The main lobby is lined with famous quotations about the free press.

Jules worked on the tenth floor, the floor below the official floor of the Tribune. He took the elevator to the tenth floor and logged in and began his normal workday. He checked in with the manager in charge and picked up his assignments for the day.

D'Angelo discussed the various issues in the Tribune building that morning. In the computer technology laboratory bullpen D'Angelo, the department manager, announced the tasks lists which were the computer team's individual responsibility.

"Remember, need updates. As you all know the tasks continue to come in."

By eight thirty everyone was in motion. Jules meandered back to his desk with a manila folder which had the latest requests from his departments. Jules was responsible for the maintenance of eight departments at the Tribune.

He considered each issue after finding his desk and opening his task list. Advertising was always a drive by. Jules had streamlined the department and found most of the issues, if there were issues, came from malware. So, Jules had created a dummy account for the Advertising department to receive and then filter out obvious malware or emails with attachments. Creating the dummy account had made life for everyone at the Tribune easier.

Jules had been asked to replicate the software and create a malware filter across all departments. Jules, of course, created the malware program, a hybrid program which others had initially utilized individually. Individually the piecemeal approach had never been robust enough to capture suspicious emails with attachments.

Jules had worked holistically around all of the department protocols and made every employee acknowledge the receipt of anything suspicious. There was a keystroke log created when files considered by the algorithm dangerous were received. Each department was mandated to click a number of boxes they deemed safe to finally open an attachment. All this happened unbeknownst to the Tribune staff. They did not need to know. They only cared that their email was scanned and deemed safe.

The most labor intense departments happened to be the Obituaries and Jobs & Work and Classified for Jules. Sometimes, Jules realized, he could go to one of those departments and be there through lunch unraveling a computer problem which had begun with one of the staff members deeming something safe and then finding the whole department quarantined.

Jules spent most of his working hours in the Obituaries, Jobs & Work, and Classified department chasing down and destroying malware worms and griffins and wyverns that were trying to break out of the system lock down. It was time consuming and essential work, but few understood or cared.

"Hey Jules, how long is this going to take?"

"Well, based on past experience," Jules always said. "Give me two hours to diagnose and clean up the computer systems. You can work but do not accept any emails with attachments until I have given the all clear."

It was just routine.

Max texted Jules. He was curious if there was a chance to meet up that night or the next. Jules texted Max back he would call him after work. Right after texting Max he texted Bethany to see if she was still good to meet him for lunch.

On his way to Breaking News Jules texted Bethany.

"You good?"

He planned not to look at his phone until eleven. He was giving Bethany some space.

Real Estate, Autos, and Breaking News were always fun departments to visit for Jules. When he was looking for a place to stay, he spoke to one of the Real Estate brokers who daily dealt with listings and they had pointed him to Logan Square. The rent was reasonable, and the location was incredibly convenient. Jules knew if he were in the market for a car the same opportunities would have been offered to him by the department manager. Everyone at the Tribune looked out for each other. It was a family atmosphere.

Tribune Archives had become a pet project of Jules. He simply was helping digitize the over one hundred years of front pages of the Chicago Tribune for the archives curated by Stephanie Feingold. The Tribune management, once they learned scanning every page of the century old Tribune onto the website might take years were more than satisfied with digitizing the front page and key pages. At present, there was a debate over essential decades and dates being fully digitized.

Jules had offered his expertise and explained there would probably need to be a set of servers dedicated to the one-hundred-year project. Though, there were one hundred years of news there were only, at present, one hundred front pages from each year that the Tribune had been published. But the project was on hold as the management stalled and battled over the idea of digitizing a full year of front pages. That would be three hundred and sixty-five front pages each year.

He stuck his head in Stephanie Feingold's office.

"We got any good news?"

"No, we are still waiting," Stephanie smiled from behind her cat eyeglasses. She was an older white woman in her fifties with shoulder length dirty blonde hair. Stephanie looked a bit like a throwback librarian, Jules always thought.

"Well, keep me informed," Jules said and stopped before he continued on his way.

"Hey Stephanie, while we are waiting can you tell me how to look up a criminal who was arrested and put in prison for attempted armed robbery," Jules smiled.

Stephanie Feingold was a slightly attractive woman in her early fifties who was starting to show her age. She had a diamond face framed by dirty blonde hair which had streaks of gray poking through. Her thin arched eyebrows sat above her light blue eyes which were perpetually behind oversized glasses that looked like they were in fashion in the sixties or seventies. Feingold dressed nicely. She had a nice shape, Jules admitted but no ass to speak of.

The day Jules asked for help Stephanie Feingold was dressed in a summer blouse that showed off her age spotted chest and ample cleavage and floral skirt.

"Well, you have a name?"

Jules nodded. He had written all the information on a 3"x 5" index card. He handed it to the archive's curator.

"How long ago?"

"Think it's not more than three years," Jules said.

Stephanie Feingold nodded. "I don't have too much to do around here, at the moment. Let me check. I'll get back to you."

"I'd appreciate it. Just curious what happened. Who was in-volved? You know the basics."

"Let me see what I dig up."

"Okay, thanks."

Jules left the Archives department and headed back to D'Angelo to report in his first half of the day. D'Angelo did not like to be disturbed when he was working and requested every tech type an update by twelve o'clock and four o'clock each day so the first night shift could keep up with the workload. Jules walked past D'Angelo's office and went to his office and typed up what he had done in the morning. It took him twenty minutes.

At eleven Jules checked his phone and saw Bethany had texted. She wanted to meet.

Jules texted her and gave her the Tribune Tower address.

At noon Bethany met Jules in the lobby for lunch.

Bethany was dressed a light blue short-sleeved polo shirt and blue jeans. On her feet were a white pair of Nike Jordan basketball sneakers. Her hair was still in her signature Mohawk, but the Mohawk was now in thick braids.

Jules smiled broadly seeing Bethany. She smiled incorrigibly as well and closed the distance and hugged and kissed him.

"Good to see you," Jules said.

"You too," Bethany responded.

"Like your hair," Jules said.

Bethany smiled. "Thank you. My auntie did it for me."

The pair left the iconic Tribune Tower and walked down Michigan Avenue and across the bridge to sit at the very busy bean.

"You want something?"

Bethany smiled. "Whatever you having?"

Bethany seemed so relaxed, Jules' thought. He walked to the closest street vendor and decided on a Chicago staple. The choices were limited.

Jules walked back to where Bethany was seated and could not help smiling. She seemed at ease. The beautiful girl dressed like she might work at Best Buy seemed to really enjoy sitting and people watching. Jules slowed his pace and just enjoyed watching Bethany sitting near the iconic bean.

Jules had two slices of pizza in hand.

"Do you ever eat anything other than fast food?"

"Of course," Jules grinned. "I just break all my rules when I am with you," Jules confessed.

"What rules?"

"I mostly have a strict diet. I make most of my own meals. Have to control what I intake. I exercise five out of seven days," Jules admitted.

"Are you trying to impress me?"

Jules smiled.

"Well, that's impressive."

Jules laughed nervously.

"What kind of meals do you make?"

Jules shook his head.

"I don't want to talk about my diet," Jules said. "I want to talk about you. I want to hear about you. I want to hang out with you."

"That's fair," Bethany smiled.

The pair ate Chicago deep dish pizza. They washed it all down with drinks from a street vendor. Jules surprises Bethany with ice cream before Jules has to go back to work.

"This on your diet?"

Jules shook his head.

"I might be bad for you, Jules," Bethany said, seriously.

"I'm a grown man, Bee," Jules said. "I can do bad all by myself."

Bethany laughed.

"Well, I have to go back to work," Jules said.

"Yeah, me too," Bethany said standing up and picking up her trash. Jules extended his hand and Bethany handed him the trash she had gathered. Jules scanned the park and found the closest trash can and headed for it. Bethany followed.

"Bee, what do you do, for work?"

"Don't laugh," Bethany smiled and leaned on Jules' arm. "I'm a secretary for one of the professors at Loyola University."

"Really?" Jules smiled.

Bethany eyed Jules for any signs of humor.

"How long you been doing that?"

"Just a year," Bethany smiled.

"Is it fun?"

"It can be," Bethany said as they walked back to the Tribune Tower. "I like it. The professor is from England. He has traveled all over the world. He is here, at the university for a few years doing research on gangsters or something. I sort of just answer the phone and type up whatever he asks me to type up." Bethany twisted her lips. "It's sort of boring but fun at the same time."

At the Tribune Tower Bethany pulled Jules back from the revolving doors.

Jules smiled, studying Bethany.

"Why are you smiling?"

"I just don't want this to end," Jules said.

Bethany nodded. "I don't want it to end either."

"Want to do something tonight?"

"Sure,"

"Okay, I get off at six. I'll call you."

"Okay," Bethany said. "I will be off a little earlier. So, I'll head home. Call me, when you're off."

The pair kissed and hugged. Bethany did not break the embrace. Jules breathed in Bethany's scent and playfully nibbled at her neck making her giggle and push him away.

"Sorry, just wanted to know if you taste as good as you look."

"Do I?"

"Not possible. You look too good," Jules smiled.

Jules was infatuated with the beauty.

Bethany shook her head. He could not stop smiling as Bethany walked down Michigan Avenue and at the taxi stand caught a taxi. He watched and waved as the taxi disappeared in the traffic headed north.

Jules turned and entered the Tribune Tower and walked to the elevator bank. He tapped the elevator and returned to his office.

On his desk were new updates he needed to address.

Of all the departments, Jules liked checking in with Breaking News. There were little computer issues there. The reporters were savvy. They understood their computers were their life blood. They did not accept email attachments unless it was from a trusted source.

Jules had made friends with a number of reporters who had issues with their computers. He was always friendly and professional. Jules helped anyone and everyone who asked for his help.

It was how he got to know the top investigative reporters Sam Arnold and Ray Hicks.

He went to the department and not seeing them at their desks went back to his office to give D'Angelo an update. As soon as he gave an update, he was asked to return to the Obituaries department and check on a possible malware situation.

An hour after he returned from the Obituaries department, he got a message from Sam Arnold. Jules read the message. Jules called Sam and confirmed what the investigator had found.

Jules wanted to call Bethany and tell her what Sam Arnold had found but he decided the discovery was not something to share over the phone. Some things were not phone conversation subjects.

An hour before Jules was to get off work, he got an email from Stephanie Feingold. Jules was writing his last update report for D'Angelo. He was less than an hour from being off work.

He read the email and skimmed her note. The email listed the court date, the conviction and the imprisonment. The thing which was fascinating were the name of the witnesses for the defense. What caught Jules' eye was a prison phone number attached.

A few minutes after receiving the email Jules got a text message from Bethany.

"Jules, I wish you were here."

'What's going on?"

Jules watched the phone for Bethany's answer.

"Nothing."

"You sure?"

Jules checked the time and decided he would call Bethany after he got off work. Before he left, he called the prison phone number Stephanie Feingold had attached. He called and waited for the connection. He waited and connected with a complete stranger. The conversation was short and sweet. The person on the other end of the phone yelled, cursed and denied everything Jules told him.

"Listen, I ain't asking you to believe me. I just don't think that it is going to be too hard to find out if I'm lying or not, even from where you are right now," Jules said.

The person on the end of the line growled and threatened Jules. He would have been surprised if he had gotten off the phone without a threat.

He hoped to get another response before he left work. Unfortunately, he did not get a response to the email or phone call before the end of the workday. So, Jules hung out for an extra thirty minutes before he headed home.

Before leaving he went up to the thank Sam and Stephanie for their assistance. Sam Arnold was a bearded stocky man with receding dark hair and a lined but friendly face. He was not a big man. He was maybe five foot seven or eight inches tall and one hundred and sixty pounds. Sam had thin eyebrows, blue eyes and a straight nose.

"Hope that information helps, Jules," Sam said.

"It didn't take you too long?"

"Not at all," Sam smiled.

"Well, I owe you for this," Jules said. "Just name it."

"Don't worry about it."

"Thanks again," Jules said and left the Breaking News department.

On the way-out Jules dropped into Archives department. Stephanie Feingold had left. He wrote a quick note to Stephanie and slipped it into her mailbox and left.

Once off work and on Michigan Avenue Jules called Bethany.

No answer.

He stood on Michigan Avenue and allowed the foot traffic to pass him as he tried to think what he should do. It was the first time Bethany had not answered his phone call. Instantly, Jules started thinking he had suffocated his crush, like Tre and Harold said. He had made Bethany realize she could do better. All sorts of ideas flitted into his mind.

Jules considered going to Bethany's house. As soon as he thought the thought, he discarded it. He could not go unannounced to Bethany's home.

He was panicky. Jules considered calling her again. He stopped himself. He had to wait.

Jules caught the el train to Logan Square. The short ride did not make Jules feel better. He was unsure what to do. He reluctantly returned home.

He turned the corner to his apartment and found Bethany on the stoop, crying.

"What happened? You okay? What's going on?"

Bethany had her hair unbraided and in two Afro puffs on either side of her heart shaped face.

"Diamond decided to kick me and my mom out of the apartment," Bethany said. Tears rolled down her cheeks. "He slapped and threatened me and told his boys I was a thot." She paused. "He let me take my mom to my aunt's, but he threatened me if I come back his boys were going to treat me like...." She trailed off.

"What?" Jules was suddenly angry. He climbed to his feet. Bethany held his hand. He looked down upon his heart shaped sweetheart. He could not leave her.

"Don't," Bethany said. She gently pulled Jules back to her seated form. He sat back down.

"What do you want me to do?"

"What do you mean?"

He shrugged. "You can stay here," Jules said. "You know that. But what do you want to do about Diamond?"

Bethany did not answer. She lowered her head in response.

"I guess I have to do what I said I would," Jules said.

"What does that mean?"

"Be the man I said I was," Jules answered.

"No, Jules, I don't want that."

"Somethings are out of our hands, Bee," Jules said.

Bethany squeezed Jules' hand and looked at him, questioningly.

"What I look like not being able to protect my girl?"

Bethany narrowed her almond shaped eyes and studied Jules. She did not speak. Instead, she reached out and pulled the solid man toward her. Bethany hung on Jules' arm.

"Just let this go," Bethany said.

Jules did not like Bethany's response. He tried not to allow his face to react, but he winced as if Bethany had hit him in his eye.

He looked away and tried to regain his composure.

"Come on, you can't just sit on the stoop, moping and crying," Jules said.

He helped Bethany to her feet and walked her into the apartment house.

They took the elevator to the fourth floor. The pair walked to the corner apartment. Jules unlocked the apartment and allowed Bethany to enter.

Jules followed, troubled, thinking what he should do.

"You hungry?"

Bethany pressed into Jules' chest and without thought he held her as she softly cried. He did not speak. He just allowed Bethany to weep and let whatever was inside of her out. Jules held onto Bethany and let her release him.

They sat on the couch. They cuddled. She held onto him like he was life itself. He listened to her breathing and tenderly wiped away her tears.

Bethany and Jules sat on the couch and after an hour she was sleeping on his shoulder.

Jules fished out his cellphone and made a couple of phone calls.

He lifted her into his arms and carried her to the bedroom. Jules deposited Bee on the bed and watched her get comfortable. He wrapped the bedsheet around her and returned to the living room. Jules prepared to leave the apartment, after writing a short note and placing the note on the coffee table.

Max was in the hall as Jules left.

"Everything okay?"

"No." Jules said. "Do me a favor Max, just sit there and hang with

Bee. Nothing too complicated. I'll be back in a bit. I just don't want her here alone."

"Yeah, yeah, yeah," Max smiled. "I got you."

"Thanks," Jules said and bounded down the stairs toward the first floor.

Chapter Eleven

At the curb sat the Escalade and Tre and Harold.

"You sure about this?"

"Sure, as I'm breathing." Jules said after he climbed into the Escalade.

Harold looked at Tre and Tre looked at Jules in the second row of the Escalade. Tre nodded. Harold handed Jules a pistol. Jules laughed at the pistol. He examined it and after Harold and Tre stopped watching him as if he might blow off his own head Jules slipped the pistol under the car seat.

The trio drove from Logan Square. They found North Milwaukee Avenue and then Touhy. They headed to Rogers Park.

Jules gave Tre directions to Bethany's apartment. They turned the corner and drove up to the apartment from the rear. They parked the Escalade under a tree.

"All I want to do is teach this fool a lesson. Me and him. No one else."

"Got you, my dude," Harold smiled. "Ain't nobody getting involved but you and this bitch ass nigger."

"We got this," Tre said slipping his machine pistol out of his stash box.

The three moved slowly through the sunset oranges and blues of the pre-night.

There were three cars parked in front of the horseshoe apartment. The familiar BMW 733i sat between two other cars. There was an older Camaro and a Chevy Blazer. Based on the cars alone there were at least three people in the apartment to contend with. Jules raised three fingers to Tre and Harold. Both the gangsters nodded, unfazed.

As they got closer to the cars Jules slowed and pointed to the thin boy dressed in loose-fitting jeans and a T-shirt leaning on the Camaro. Tre swung wide and into the street out of the eyesight of the boy.

Harold and Jules kept walking slowly forward. The boy looked and suddenly became alert. Before the boy could decide what to do Tre stepped out of the dark and behind him.

"Don't do anything stupid and I won't do anything stupid," Tre advised. He braced the thin boy and disarmed him. "How many people in the apartment?"

"Four," the boy said.

"Which car is yours?"

"This one," he said. He was pressed against the Camaro. "Pop the trunk."

Jules and Harold continued forward.

At the apartment door was another kid. Harold and Jules walked past the apartment door.

"Hey, man, you got a cigarette?"

The kid, tall and angular with bushy eyebrows and a pinched expression shook his head. When Harold had asked the question, the boy had stepped down the step with a blank look on his face. Harold seeing the boy step down turned and lifted his Uzi toward the boy. The surprised boy on the steps lifted his hands and immediately, Harold gestured for the boy to put his hands down.

"Don't be stupid," Harold said. Harold stepped forward and disarmed the boy. He pushed the boy toward Tre. Tre smiled. Tre snatched off the boy's web belt and fashioned a handmade hand restraint. He restrained the second boy and pushed the boy toward the Camaro.

Tre deposited the second boy and moved from the Camaro to the front of the apartment.

"There's three left," Jules said.

"Got it," Harold said.

"How we handle this?"

"Simple," Tre said. He reached out and rang the doorbell.

Tre stood back. Harold braced for trouble. Jules stepped back and beside Harold.

A horse faced boy with a gold chain around his neck peeked out the door. He was dressed like the others in a T-shirt, loose-fitting jeans and Nike basketball sneakers. Harold beckoned him toward him, the Uzi leveled at the boy in the doorway.

"Diamond, can you come out here," Jules growled.

Diamond and another boy appeared on the doorstep. The boy next to Diamond was an oval faced boy with an overbite. He had bushy eyebrows, a broad nose and thick lips. He had a gold chain around his neck. He was wearing a gray T-shirt, the only distinction from the other three boys they had run into.

Diamond smiled and pushed out of the apartment, fearless.

"You got a death wish?"

"Naw, nigger, no one got a death wish," Tre growled. "But you act a fool and we will be bucking up in this bitch until we go click-click."

"Who the fuck are you?"

Tre looked at Jules.

"Remember me, Diamond?"

"Yeah, you that roach that I tried to crush but guess did not crush completely."

"You some big man? You beat up Bethany?" Jules seethed.

"That's what this is about?"

"Naw, motherfucker, that ain't what this is about. This is about after this, you leaving Bethany and her mother alone, for good."

Diamond smiled. He was not an ugly man. He was honey colored, much lighter than Jules. He had loose wavy curls which signified Diamond's past was checkered long before his birth. Diamond had a pinky ring. He looked a little like a caricature of what someone might think of a street hustler if they had grown up in the seventies. He was dressed in some garish designed silk shirt which had skulls and daggers dominating the sides and back. He was wearing some designer jeans which had to cost a couple of hundred dollars. On his feet were the newest pair of Nike Jordan basketball sneakers.

"You know I thought to end you," Diamond pointed out. "But I ain't that guy anymore. I got bigger plans than you. I'm a business-man. I'm stacking money. No one got time for you and this bull-shit."

Jules listened.

"I had them toss you over the railing with the rest of the gar-bage. Remember, bitch ass, don't nobody sneak up on me and take what I don't want taken."

Diamond gnashed his teeth.

"You want Bethany?" Diamond laughed. He pinched his nose and smirked. "She's my bitch. She owes me bank. Pay her freight. Twenty-five large. She's yours. Otherwise, she's mine to push around and rough up a little to remind her that nobody rides for free."

"You rough her up a little?" Jules seethed. "You rough her up a bit to remind her—you asshat--nobody owns nobody anymore," Jules said balling his fists as he spoke. "We ain't the fucking op-pressors! We are better than that!"

Jules stopped himself. He was seeing red. For a moment he wished he had taken the gun Harold had offered. He might have killed Diamond then and there.

Diamond Martin smirked. The Rogers Park gangster rubbed his lip and watched Jules like a cat toying with a mouse. It, his look, infuriated Jules. The smugness which Diamond exuded got under

Jules' skin.

"Your cape is showing," Diamond joked.

"I came here to make you understand that Bethany and you are done. She's done being scared of you."

"How you going to stop that, playboy?"

Jules shook his head. "If I have to beat the black off you to make you understand that your show is over then so be it. But at the end of the day, I'm here to tell you that Bethany and her mother are done with you."

"That bitch owes me a twenty-five large."

"Where did you get that number?"

Diamond was enjoying the conversation. "Where did I get that number? That skank has been nibbling at my cash for nearly a year to pay for her mom's care and to take care of the rent."

Tre and Harold were watching the streets.

"My dude, we can't sit here all night."

"Make shit happen," Tre growled.

"Right," Jules said. "No, bogus benefactor, Bethany don't owe you shit," Jules said.

"Street rules, pussy whipped nigger, is in play," Diamond noted.

"Street rules? You a two-bit gangster and a lousy conman. You a two-bit gangster because you ain't shit. You one of those barking dogs behind the fence. Open the fence and you pretend like the fence is still there."

Harold and Tre looked at each other and back at Jules and Diamond.

"You tricked an old woman and her daughter to believe you were their savior only to find out that they let the devil in their house, instead."

"What you talking about?" Diamond hissed.

"You know the medical bills you so graciously tell Bethany and her mother you pay are really not paid by you," Jules said. "I did some research and found out you ain't paying for shit."

"What you saying little nigger?"

"You a liar," Jules said.

"Don't lie on me."

"I don't need to lie. Facts are facts. Truth is truth."

Diamond smiled at the two thugs who had been disarmed and were guarded by Harold and Tre.

"This fool is crazy. Everyone knows I pay Bethany's bills because of my love for her brother."

"You know I know people," Jules said.

Diamond scoffed. "Shit you saying is stupid."

"I did a little research and found out you lied to Bethany and her mother. Somehow you intercepted the billing and told them you were over the payments. But her mother has an insurance policy in place to pay for her medical. The thing is that would be bad enough because she has dementia but the worse is that you lied to Bethany's brother Angel too. He ain't too happy about that."

"What?"

"Before he went away, he squirreled away some money for his mom and you were suppose to use it to help Bethany and her mom. You lied to them and pretended to be helping them when you are doing the most."

Diamond laughed. "That's crazy shit," the Rogers Park gangster smiled and for the first time his smile seemed a little tremulous.

"I don't know when this lie began but it's a lie no matter what," Jules said.

Diamond looked at his underlings. They looked at him. Diamond rubbed his chin. The two thugs seemed shaken.

"Angel knows. Bethany knows. Everybody knows." Jules refocused. "Your bullshit is exposed."

Diamond stepped down a step and Jules took a step back ready for the inevitable.

"The sad part of this lie is that you twisted, a good thing, into a warped and evil thing."

"You don't know shit," Diamond Martin said.

"So, do I have to beat the black off you or is this shit over," Jules asked.

Diamond stood big and bad but not moving. He seemed to be thinking and mulling over all the details Jules had offered. The Rogers Park gangster, the mean mugging, bad boy, was quiet. He seemed stunned and unsure.

Jules did not smile though he wanted to. He was prepared for the attack from Diamond. He expected it to come from frustration or anger. Yet, nothing happened. Jules took a step back. He studied the trio in the front of the apartment.

No fight came. No yell. No scream. Nothing. Instead, he looked at Tre and Harold for direction.

"Think we rolling," said Tre, who was the first to start to back up.

Harold reached out and pushed Jules toward the cars.

Jules looked back and for a moment felt confident enough to

smile. He watched as Diamond and his two flunkies just stood there. Diamond was looking down at the ground.

Chapter Twelve

The Escalade skated from the rear of Roger Sullivan high school unhampered. Tre handled the large SUV expertly. They drove looking for one or all of the Rogers Park gangsters to follow but no one followed. Harold, every minute they drove, looked back looking for a car to be following.

"Jules, this is not good," Harold said, looking back.

"What you mean?"

"I mean, they ain't following," Harold Waller said.

"I don't get it."

Harold just shook his head and went silent.

"What am I missing?"

Tre drove and did not speak immediately.

"The way this shit breaks down is that you shut down shit or it festers and comes back. That Diamond character is one of those sneaky motherfuckers that ain't above letting you think that shit is over and when you ain't thinking about it no more he comes in guns blazing," Harold said.

"But he didn't step up when I called him out," Jules said.

They were navigating the backstreets which took them passed the high school and toward Newgard Avenue. Harold was looking back as they got to the first busy street. Still no one was following.

"They don't see you as a threat, my dude," Harold said.

Jules looked confused.

"No, I figured out that he was full of shit," Jules countered. "The game is up. He can't threaten Bethany or her mother anymore."

Harold shook his head. Tre was wheeling the Escalade. Once on Newgard Avenue Tre slipped his machine pistol away and looked back at Jules. Harold hid his Uzi and looked out the car window, silent.

"So, the way this ends, is you and your girl are relaxing somewhere and up walks that nigger and he goes all Tony Montana on your ass," Tre said.

"Or, he tries to let you feel like shit is squashed and you know that it ain't squashed. So, he back at the camp plotting and planning ways to take you off the block. And you swing by one day and think shit's cool and again he goes all Tony Montana on your unprepared ass."

Jules sat in the second row of the Cadillac Escalade and tried to make sense of what Tre and Harold were saying. He replayed what had just happened.

"What was I suppose to do?"

Tre looked back and shook his head. He kept driving.

"You been in the green grass too long," Tre said.

"What's that suppose to mean?"

Tre just shook his head.

Harold leaned out the window and then pulled his head back in. He adjusted in his seat. Harold took a deep breath.

"Jules, you know that this ain't over. Right?"

Tre was driving the Escalade and making his way back toward Ashland Avenue. Harold rolled down his window and let the warm air into the SUV. Jules waited for Tre or Harold to ask for the pistol back but neither did. He had other thoughts on his mind.

"What do you mean?"

Harold looked back. He chuckled.

Jules looked at Tre, curious. He slowly looked at Harold, but Harold only shook his head, seemingly more concerned about what he saw on the street.

"What?"

Harold looked out the window again as the Escalade slowed.

"You can't think that the Freakyville bitch ass nigger gonna let you call him out and not seek..." Tre trailed off as they rolled to a stop light. At the stop light Tre looked left and right and ahead for any sneak attack.

Harold looked and watched Tre checking his surroundings. "Retaliation," Harold finished. "Shit is not over until one of you stomps a mudhole in the other."

Jules was suddenly confused. He looked at Harold and Tre. "Naw, things are done," Jules said. "I gave him the chance. He didn't take it."

"It was kind of on you, my dude," Harold said.

"No. No. No. I called him out. He had opportunity. He chose not to do anything," Jules noted. "Shit is over, far as I'm concerned."

"Far as your concerned," Tre said accelerating and moving the Escalade down the busy street. "Fuck Jules, you been away too long. You know that shit ain't over until one of you shows dominance over the other, whatever that looks like." Tre added, "Talk is just talk. We handle things with our hands, knives or guns."

Jules sat in the second row of the Escalade and let what Tre was saying sink in. He had given Diamond ample opportunity to attack but he had not. Instead, the Rogers Park gangster had hesitated. Maybe, Jules thought, Diamond would use the fact Harold and Tre had burners and would have chopped them down as an excuse later on.

"What do I have to do?"

"You and that fucker going to have to come to blows," Tre added as the light changed and the Escalade slid toward the Stevenson underpass and what would signal their exit from Rogers Park. "One of you gonna have to leak the other or shit will...fester."

Jules did not say anything. He did not know what to say. He wanted to argue he had outsmarted Diamond and it meant things were over. He had the higher moral ground. Diamond was in the wrong and it meant there was nothing left to prove. Jules held all the cards, but Jules knew innately what the two gangsters said was true.

They were still a few blocks from the Stevenson Freeway underpass. Harold looked back and smiled. Tre, driving smirked.

"So, what now?"

"You asking?"

"Yeah, man, I'm asking," Jules said.

"Well," Tre smiled. "If it was me, I wouldn't want some Freakyville wannabe plotting and planning on ending me. I would turn my slap happy ass around and go and finish what I started."

Harold nodded.

Jules bit his lower lip, thinking.

They were still on Ashland Avenue. Jules adjusted in the back seat and saw they were maybe a few blocks from the Stevenson Freeway underpass.

"See the problem is that you done got soft and I mean that in the nicest way. You done moved away. You got out of all the chaos. You wised up, college boy," Harold chuckled. "When we was living off Garfield Park shit like this was just normal. You have beef with someone then you sought them out and handled it then and there. If they beat your ass, then you knew that the next time your stupid ass was going to get your ass beat again. Rules of the street." Harold turned and looked at Jules sadly. "Now you all college educated and working at that newspaper and thinking that you can deal with a street nigger like you can deal with a mad or upset Brad or a Chad or Karen." Harold shook his head. "Fuck that. We don't believe in the cancel culture in the streets except when you cancelling tickets."

The Escalade rolled down Ashland Avenue toward the underpass.

"What you going to do?"

"Fuck," was all Jules could say.

Tre and Harold smiled like it was Christmas in response.

"It's gotta be done," Harold said.

"Suppose you're right," Jules said reluctantly.

Tre looked right and then left and turned the Escalade into the driveway of a strip mall which displayed a check cashing place, a restaurant, a liquor store and several smaller businesses. Tre drove through the small parking lot and out of the opposite driveway and back toward Rogers Park.

The Escalade rolled to a stop again under the Rogers Park tree of the apartment house where the trio had been earlier. Harold had his Uzi in hand again. Tre had his machine pistol. Jules, now, had the nine-millimeter pistol Harold had given him in his hand as he walked to the front of the horseshoe apartment house. The three vehicles: Camaro, BMW and Chevy Blazer were still parked in front. Jules noted there was another car on the side of the Blazer, a blue Audi.

"This is a bad idea," Harold said under his breath.

"Yeah, I think so," Tre agreed.

"How the hell you going to tell me that this is a bad idea and I'm seconds from cancelling this fucker?"

"Never thought you had the balls to turn around," Harold smiled.

"Let alone, say, "I give two fucks about this motherfucker" before," Tre said.

"Yeah," Jules agreed.

The three approached the apartment house.

"We got your back," Tre smiled.

"Yeah, our boy has grown up," Harold smiled.

Jules shook his head and stepped around the corner of the apartment house and took in the sight of Diamond, Cole, peanut boy, bird, and the three others he had seen earlier.

He lifted his pistol toward Diamond. The seven Rogers Park gangsters reached for their guns but at the same time Harold came around the corner of the apartment house with his Uzi leveled at the seven gathered on the three-stair stoop. Tre was the last to arrive and aimed his machine pistol toward the three gangsters who thought they might slip out of the line of fire.

"Keep your hands where I can see them," Harold barked. "If you foolish, I might have to be foolish all over you. Hands up."

"Hands up, niggers," Tre growled. He braced the two closest to him and threw their guns on the lawn. He retrieved a switchblade from one of the three and pocketed it. He pushed them back toward the others. Everyone had their hands up except Diamond and Cole.

Harold kept the Uzi leveled on the group as Tre disarmed the group slowly.

"It's on you, my dude," Harold said when Tre looked at Harold satisfied, he had disarmed everyone.

"Okay, Diamond, looks like this shit between you and me ain't over," Jules said.

Diamond smirked as an answer.

"You suppose to be all sorts of smart, but we can't handle this here," Diamond said.

Tre nodded. Harold nodded. Jules just looked.

"What you suggest?"

"Over there, on the basketball court. Ain't nobody there to witness," Diamond said.

"Let's roll."

The unarmed Freakyville boys led the way to the basketball court. The walk was short. They entered through an opening barely visible in the chain-link fencing surrounding the school. The basketball court sat on the edge of the high school. At that time of day there was no one outside or around.

Diamond stopped at the top of the court and smiled maliciously at Jules, Harold and Tre despite the fact the two were armed and dangerous.

"Okay, stupid fuck, bring your A game and let's settle this shit."

Diamond looked at Harold and Tre.

"They are just here to make sure none of your boys get ideas if I beat the snot out of you."

"Fair fight?"

"Fair as you and I get," Jules smirked.

"You know I told you that I thought to end you a couple of nights before," Diamond pointed out. "But I was trying not be that guy anymore." Diamond smiled and showed off his four gold incisors. "I guess that shit is out the door now." Diamond looked at Cole. "He came back for an ass whooping."

Tre took the pistol from Jules and Diamond stepped forward craning his neck and loosening his shoulder muscles in preparation for the bare-knuckle fight between him and Jules.

Jules balled his fists and prepared for the gangster's attack. Jules took a deep breath and prepared for Diamond.

"You know, little nigger, the first night you overstepped I was trying to be kinder. But you know that I thought about popping you, but didn't," Diamond said as he reached the free throw line of the basketball court which disappeared back toward the still and silent basketball hoop. "Suppose this is my fault. If I would have popped you three nights ago, I wouldn't be here now."

Diamond jumped and threw a rocket of a punch at Jules that might have knocked him off his feet. Jules slid back and dodged the punch. He watched as Diamond flew past him.

Diamond landed and turned on his heels and came running back at Jules, this time, low and with his hands out. It seemed as if Diamond was trying to grab and catch hold.

Jules spun out of the reach of Diamond. Diamond was thickly built across his shoulders and chest. He looked like a wooden battering ram. For all of his muscles, Diamond was slower.

The two circled one another and the Rogers Park gangsters slowly circled Diamond and Jules. The Rogers Park gangsters watched and egged on Diamond.

Harold and Tre watched and allowed the two to fight undisturbed.

Twice Diamond grabbed hold of Jules only to be punched relentlessly away by the jackhammers attached to Jules strongly built shoulders.

Diamond was the first to draw blood to the delight of the Rogers Park gangsters as the two collided and Diamond landed a glancing blow that cut Jules' lower lip.

Jules watched and measured Diamond's attacks watching him dive in and retreat looking for a wild swing to capitalize on. It had been Jules' wild swing at Diamond which allowed the Rogers Park tough to draw blood. It was a mistake he was not going to make again.

The two fighters circled one another and under the shouts and screams of murder Diamond rushed forward and unable to grab Jules the wooden battering ram began to retreat. Jules pounced on the retreating Diamond, driving him to the ground. On the ground Diamond seemed to have an advantage. Yet, it was Jules who came up on top of Diamond dropping fist bombs from on high.

"Get up," someone screamed.

"Get up or he'll kill you," someone else called.

Diamond twisted and struggled and desperately fought to his feet. Suddenly Diamond was bleeding from his nose. He wiped at his nose, but the blood did not stop.

Jules circled. The blood drip from Diamond's nose encouraged Jules. Jules for the first time went on the attack. He stepped forward and threw a soft left followed by and rocket of a right. The right glanced off Diamond's cheek as he retreated.

Diamond ran into one of his henchmen and ricocheted off him. Diamond jacked his arms and balled his fists, ready for battle. The Rogers Park gangster prowled the inner circle looking for an opening.

"Bitch ass nigger," Diamond screamed and jumped at Jules. Jules easily avoided Diamond. Diamond skidded to a stop by Cole, and in the moment, he got close Cole reached out and palmed Diamond a knife.

Diamond smiled from ear-to-ear and twirled the blade expertly in his hand. Harold and Tre seeing Diamond was armed with a knife looked at each other.

Diamond rushed forward with evil in his eyes. He smirked as he nearly cut Jules. At the last moment, Jules had avoided being cut.

"Tre, get our boy a pig sticker," Harold said. Tre looked from Harold to Jules and back to the gangsters watching the fight. Tre tapped his back pocket and fished out the knife he had taken from the Rogers Park gangster earlier.

At the moment Diamond ran past Jules and missed his throat only to cut him across his ear. Jules winced and stumbled as Diamond slid to a stop a few feet away.

Diamond spun and seeing an opportunity pounced on the bleeding Jules. Jules braced and turned Diamond and the knife away from him without harm.

Tre pushed into the circle. He appeared on the edge of the fight circle with another blade. He opened it and threw the blade onto the court where it clattered and tumbled to a stop just a few feet from Jules. Diamond seeing the blade on the court crouched and smiled.

Jules reached out and retrieved the blade and stood up cautiously. He narrowed his dark brown eyes at the cause of the pain. Diamond smiled.

The two circled each other. The Rogers Park crew were waiting for someone to die. Tre and Harold waited as well.

"You know I was raised on the streets," Diamond said as he jumped forward, nearly stabbing Jules in the heart. Jules retreated, narrowly escaping the attack.

Diamond circled. He hefted the blade high and then switched hands. With each step he seemed to be looking for the right moment to end the fight.

Jules circled too. Jules moved just a little slower as his cut thigh darkened his jeans with blood. Each step on that leg made him wince just a little more.

"Fighting is all I know how to do," Diamond growled. "I ain't the strongest. I ain't the meanest. I'm just the one who watches and sees what others don't do and take advantage."

Diamond feigned an attack to the left and spun to the right of Jules. Jules lifted his arm too slowly and Diamond nicked his forearm, cutting him.

Jules pulled his arm back and groaned. His forearm was bleeding from the cut Diamond gave him.

"Figure you dead, little nigger, you just don't know it yet."

The pair continued to circle one another. The fight circle was tight and suddenly the noise fell away. Jules moved to the left. Diamond moved to the right.

Jules took a deep breath and concentrated. He let Diamond rush forward and as he had before when he got close, he reached out and tried to stab Jules. This time Diamond aimed for his heart and swung up and toward Jules' face, in an attempt to blind him.

Jules reached out and blocked Diamond's knife hand with his bleeding forearm. Diamond's blade went flying. Before Diamond could recover Jules stepped forward and grabbed Diamond by his skull and daggers silk shirt front and stepped forward and stabbed Diamond just under his arm pit.

Jules stood bleeding from his ear and forearm and waited. Diamond pushed Jules away. Jules' bleeding slid back, holding the bloody switchblade. Diamond tilted forward and crumbled on the basketball court holding his side. The fight was over.

The first to break the circle from the Rogers Park crew was

Cole. Behind him came the peanut boy with a swollen right eye.

"Shit's squashed," Tre announced.

Harold leveled the Uzi at the Rogers Park crew.

"We done here," Tre added.

Jules, Harold and Tre looked at Cole.

Everyone near Cole paused. They looked at the man in charge now that Diamond was unable to lead. Cole stared at the three and nodded.

"Next time we popping caps," Cole said.

"Ain't no next time," Tre said. "This is over. We out."

Harold reached out and pushed Jules away from the Rogers Park boys. Jules and Harold were moving away from the Rogers Park crew looking at their fallen leader. Tre was gesturing for the two and moving from the basketball court and to the side of the high school. The trio moved silently. The only noise was their breathing and feet scraping the tarmac.

Tre holding his machine pistol watched as Jules and Harold push past him.

"Keep going," Tre said.

"Drop the knife," Harold said noticing Jules still had the bloody weapon in his hand.

Jules dropped the switchblade on the side of the high school building.

Tre guarded the rear as the three headed for the chain link fence and the nearly invisible exit. The last thing that Jules saw as Harold guided him away was the Rogers Park gangsters gathered around Diamond.

Chapter
Thirteen

The drive in the Escalade from Rogers Park, for the second time, was a lot different than the first time. Jules was bleeding. Harold was sitting next to Jules trying to bandage his friend. Tre, ever the driver, was driving and every minute or two looking in the rearview or sideview mirror for anyone following.

The first few minutes in the Escalade were tense and quiet. Jules was bleeding from his ear and forearm, but he did not seem to feel the pain. He attributed it to adrenalin. He leaned back in the leather interior and closed his eyes.

Jules reached out and blocked Diamond's knife hand with his bleeding forearm. Diamond's blade went flying. Before Diamond could recover Jules stepped forward and grabbed Diamond by his shirt front and stepped forward and stabbed Diamond just under his arm pit.

Jules stood bleeding from his ear and forearm waited. Diamond pushed Jules away. Jules' bleeding slid back, holding the bloody switchblade. Diamond tilted forward and crumbled on the basketball court holding his side.

Jules opened his eyes. He was still in the Escalade with Harold and Tre. He was still bleeding.

"What now?"

"What you mean?"

Jules had blood on his hands. He was bleeding from his forearm and ear. Harold was sitting next to Jules and reached back behind the seat and pulled a shop towel. Harold tossed the towel to Jules.

"Press that on your ear."

Harold fished behind the second row and found another shop towel.

"Let me wrap this around your arm."

Harold, no nurse, tied the shop towel tightly around Jules' forearm.

"Damn, man, that hurts," Jules reminded. "I was stabbed."

"Toughen the fuck up," Harold joked.

Jules was pressing the other shop towel to his ear. He shook his head in disbelief. He had killed Diamond Martin. Diamond Martin was dead because of Jules. Jules looked up saddened.

"What do we do now?"

"*We?*" Harold looked at Jules curiously.

"Yeah," Jules said wincing as he pressed the shop towel against his forearm.

"*We* don't do shit. I mean, if you want to, I guess you can call in the fight and let the CPD swing by and get the whole flashing light thing going." Harold said as he tore the shop towel in two and wiped his hand with one of the halves. He gave the other half to Jules. Harold started wiping the blood off his hands.

"Me, I don't do anything," Tre said from behind the steering wheel.

"Everyone that was there ain't got no reason to call the police," Harold said. "They ain't going to drop dime on you if that is what you're asking."

"That's not what I was asking," Jules said, his voice a little louder than he intended.

"What you asking?"

Jules did not have the words to express what he was feeling. He opened his mouth, and nothing came out immediately. He took a breath.

"That's it?"

"That's it, my dude," Harold smiled. "Every week there are a grip of deaths in the city. No one in the city cares. So, having a piece of shit like that gangster taking off the street ain't nobody gonna care. Ain't about to have anybody crying. Everybody wins."

Harold paused. Tre drove the Escalade deftly.

"Don't seem right," Jules said.

Tre chuckled. "Remember what I told you about being too soft," Tre laughed.

"Yeah, I was thinking that too," Harold said.

Jules shook his head.

"Shit's over," Tre said.

"Yeah, shit's over. The street made that nigger. The street took that nigger," Harold smirked.

Jules listened and tried to comprehend what Tre and Harold were trying to say to him.

"Wait," Jules said, his head felt like it was spinning. He was dabbing the shop towel against his ear.

"What?"

"The street didn't take him," Jules said plainly, through clenched teeth. "I did."

"Same thing, my dude," Harold concluded.

"I ain't the street," Jules stated.

"You ain't the street. I ain't the street. But the street made us all."

"We all had moms and loved ones, soft boy," Tre smiled.

"But the street has a way of using us to get things done," Harold said.

The Escalade fell quiet.

"So, what?"

"So, nothing," Harold said pressing the towel against Jules' thigh.

"Do you think I killed him?"

"Don't go there," Tre said from the front of the Escalade. "Better not to dwell on shit like that." He paused. "You don't want that weight on you."

"Do you want me to answer that?" Harold asked. "Seriously?"

Jules shook his head, no. He struggled.

"So now we just... what?"

"Go on living," Harold snickered.

"I'm suppose to live with this," Jules asked.

"What's the alternative?"

"So, you live with this...weight?"

Harold nodded. Tre nodded. Jules shook his head.

Jules looked at his forearm. It had stopped bleeding. He looked down at the shop towel he had been using to stop the bleeding on his ear.

"Hell, man, we all live with something," Tre said.

Jules looked at Tre. He gave Harold a side glance. Harold studied Jules evenly.

Jules wanted to ask: "What you living with?" But he knew better. The pair of gangsters had grown up with Jules. Their lives were intertwined. There was little any of the three did not know about the others. They were close friends.

"How you live with this?"

"It ain't nothing to live with," Harold said. "It's what we get past."

"We all got burdens to bear, Jules," Tre said.

"It don't seem right," Jules said.

Tre scoffed.

"Ain't shit we living with fair," Tre said. "You know us. We've struggled."

Jules fell silent. He sat in the back of the Escalade and recalled all the trauma that they had experienced living off Garfield. They had been kids and for a short period of time been immune to the harsh realities of life. They had grown and then suddenly life had barged in.

Tre had been, like Jules and Harold, an only male child living with his mother in the apartment complex off Garfield Park. For

Tre, it was his mother and his two sisters. For Harold it was his mother and baby brother.

Tre was the oldest and his two sisters were two years behind him. They all had different daddies. Tre never knew his dad. He knew his mother's boyfriend and he had nearly killed him when his sister told him about some of her mother's boyfriend's bad behavior. Tre had talked it over with Harold and Jules and they had agreed his mother's boyfriend was a creep.

"I should kill that freak for trying something on my sister," Tre had told Harold and Jules.

"Tell your mother," Harold offered.

"Tell the cops," Jules said.

Tre had listened and seemed to calm down. Harold and Jules felt good about helping Tre out of a difficult situation. They figured that the creep would be on notice and the creepiness stop.

Yet, Tre was not yet legal when he confronted his mother's boyfriend in a parking lot and the next day the man who said he loved Tre's mother was dead. Harold and Jules had known Tre was going to meet the creep. They did not talk about what had happened. They didn't want to know.

The same was true of Harold. Baby was in a gang by junior high school and on the streets before he was seventeen, Jules knew. His younger brother, Benny, was this goofy kid who liked video games and comic books. Harold had not paid attention and somehow Benny got hooked on crack in the neighborhood they grew up in.

"It was my fault," Harold told Jules once. "I should have been watching out for my baby brother better."

For a year Harold tried to get Benny to kick the dope. For a year Tre and Jules watched Harold being turned inside out because Benny just did not want to release the dragon which was destroying him.

Those two moments for Tre and Harold had made them the hard men they had become today, Jules realized. They had been friends. They had run around in the same apartment complex. They laughed and joked. Then, one day, things changed. Harold was the first to move out. He was, whenever he came back to the neighborhood, with his gang.

Tre, likewise, moved out of the apartment and looked out for the three women in his life. He came by the apartment often to check on his mother. His sisters had moved out and had boyfriends. One worked at Saks on Michigan Avenue. One worked in the ticket office of the Chicago Theater.

Jules thought about all of this as the Escalade turned on Newgard and rolled toward the north.

The SUV moved as if it was on rails. The spacious SUV's interior was as quiet as a library, Jules thought absently. He looked to Harold then to Tre.

"So, that's it?" Jules asked.

Tre drove and did not speak immediately.

"I don't know what to tell you Jules," Tre finally said. "Things ain't always fair. We been on the streets most of our lives. We have seen friends gunned down. We have had shoot outs. People close to us been murked." Tre paused. "We live with things that would kill others." Tre slowed as he came to a stop light. He looked left and right and behind him. "It's what we do."

"So?" Jules asked.

Harold shook his head. "I get it, my dude. I get it. You want something to make you feel like things are going to be all right." Harold twisted his lips on his face, thinking. "The best I can do is say that ain't no cop going to come looking for you. Ain't going to be no crying mama on the TV begging you to give yourself up. This," Harold waved to the back of the Cadillac Escalade. "This is nothing new."

Jules looked at Harold, questioning.

Harold paused, wiping the blood off his hands. "This ain't NCIS or True Crime or any of that shit. There ain't no TV commercials going to advertise soap or whatnot." Harold sneered. "Every day we struggle because they want us to struggle."

"They make us struggle," Tre said from the driver's seat.

"The game is fixed, my dude," Harold continued. "We can't win. They herded us into ghettos and piled us up on top of each other and then pretended to wonder why there is so much crime in our areas. Shit is just wrong."

"But," Jules began.

"But shit has been like this forever?"

"But," Jules began.

"We have to do better? We the problem? What you gonna say?" Harold spat.

"But, are we killers?"

"Jules, killers are born or trained," Harold smiles. "We weren't born killers. We were made killers by the fucked-up system that makes us monsters, criminals and victims."

"Monsters?"

"Yeah, that is why the police, police us."

"They think we monsters, Jules," Tre said. "They call us criminals too."

"How are we victims?"

"How are we *not* victims, my dude?" Harold said with a shake of the head. "They stole us from the motherland. They enslaved us for four hundred years. We are victims every day, all day."

"This shit has been fucked up from the word go," Tre said.

"We ain't gotta lot of choices, my dude," Harold said. "It's legal for the cops to kill us. We ain't gotta be doing shit and they can kill us and not go to jail. So, they don't try to get to know us. To them we are all criminals. They just waiting to shoot us down."

"Yeah, but we ain't worrying about the cops trying to figure shit out down here, Jules," Tre scoffed. "They ain't about to stop us. They don't care about us. They ain't got an interest in finding out what happened. They ain't going to make you come in."

Harold smiled. "Yeah, this ain't Arlington Heights. You didn't beat the shit out of Biff or Todd. So, no muss, no fuss."

"They ain't gonna...," Jules began only to trail off.

"Shit don't work like that here. All his boys were there. They the only ones that could drop dime and that ain't in their best interest."

"But," Jules said.

"Let it go, Jules," Tre said. "Swallow that shit like all the other shit that we deal with every day."

"Every day," Harold said, with a knowing nod.

Jules fell silent.

"Yeah, I heard of these people that they call the *shit eaters*,"

Harold smiled. "I think that is what we are. Shit eaters. We eat shit every day at the hands of motherfuckers that we are smarter than, stronger than, harder than but they happen to have been given a four-hundred-year head start on us because they are melatonin challenged."

"What *we* did," Jules began, only to stop. "What *I* did ain't got nothing to do with white and black."

"You see, that's where you're wrong, my dude. Everything has to do with black and white."

Tre was wheeling the Escalade smoothly on the busy street. He turned onto Ashland Avenue and drove with the flow of traffic. Once on Ashland Avenue Tre adjusted his machine pistol on his lap and looked back at Jules and Harold.

"You see us rolling," Tre sneered. "We three bad ass black motherfuckers. Right?" Tre pointed to a police car pulling out of a strip mall. "See them, they are unwanted in our neighborhoods." Tre paused. "You know that police are here to police us not protect and serve us. They protect and serve everyone but us."

"Yeah, they created the police to police us," Harold chirped beside Jules. "That's some cold shit."

"They ain't here for us. They are just here to make sure we stay here and not in Bolingbrook or Arlington Heights. They got a cold job," Tre said as he drove. "Me, I always want to talk to the black cop. You know those motherfuckers have to have a twisted perspective."

Jules did not argue. He did not have the energy to argue. Jules just sat in the second row of the Cadillac Escalade and tried to make sense of what Tre and Harold were saying. He replayed what had just happened. He had killed Diamond Martin.

There has to be consequences to the action, Jules reckoned.

"Something's gonna happen," Jules said.

"Listen, Jules, this is our world," Harold said again gesturing around him. "In this world things don't work the same way as the world you live in." Harold looked at his friend and added, "We the only ones that care about what happened. Ain't nobody about to spend any extra time trying to figure out what caused some nobody punk to be stabbed in Rogers Park."

"Shit's over," Tre said looking up at the street signs and turning onto North Milwaukee Avenue. "Live with it. Don't live with it. Turn yourself in, if you feeling some kind of way about it. Just keep our names out of your mouth."

Tre turned onto Armitage Avenue he slowed and made one more right turn onto Jules' block. The ride ended with Jules climbing out of the Escalade.

"Where am I dropping you Aich?"

"Just take me to my car."

"Be cool, Jules," Harold said. "Just swallow that shit with all the other shit you've been forced to swallow all your life. Ain't nothing different today than yesterday or tomorrow."

Harold climbed into the passenger seat of the Escalade and Tre nodded and pulled away from the curb.

Chapter
Fourteen

Jules looked up at the sky and it wasn't brighter or darker than it had been the day before. He looked down the sidewalk and the cars did not appear to be darker or lighter either. Jules looked down and saw that the cut on his thigh was still leaking.

He headed to his Graystone apartment building. Jules climbed gingerly up the steps to his apartment door and entered. He checked his forearm and the bleeding had stopped for the moment. His thigh was still a little tender.

Jules moved carefully to the elevator bank and called for the elevator.

In the quiet lobby Jules tried to see if the lobby was different. Were the chairs and couch different? The stairs which led to the second floor did not appear to have changed either.

Jules entered the elevator and punched his floor. The elevator's mirrors were still the same, Jules smiled. Things had not radically and irrevocably changed, at least, Jules' thought as he climbed out of the elevator and made his way to his apartment.

Before he could unlock the apartment door it opened and there was Max dressed in loose-fitting jeans, gym shoes and a short-sleeved collared shirt. Max looked wild-eyed and about to scream when he saw Jules in the doorway.

"Don't tell me," Jules said.

"She's gone," Max confessed. "I just turned around for a minute, maybe ten and whoosh," Max continued.

Jules shook his head. He stepped into the apartment and then paused looking at the couch. The note was missing.

"How long?"

"Maybe ten, fifteen minutes tops," Max said. He looked around nervously. "She said that she was going to take a shower. I told her I would order something to eat while I waited." Max looked like a lost puppy. "I ordered some food and was waiting for it to arrive when I noticed she was gone."

Max stopped and noticed Jules holding a shop towel on his forearm.

"What happened to you?"

"I had a little accident."

Max walked Jules to the small bathroom and bandaged his longtime friend.

"So, you going to tell me what's going on?"

Jules looked at Max and shook his head.

"Some stuff you don't need to know. Just suffice it to say that I needed you to come and watch my girl," Jules said. He added, "And not *lose* her."

Max nodded.

"These cuts look like they came from a knife," Max said looking at the cut on Jules' ear and forearm.

Jules did not say anything as Max bandaged his forearm.

"Okay, so you playing the strong and silent hero?"

"Yeah, suppose I am," Jules smiled.

"It's a bit of a stretch, Jules," Max chuckled.

"Yeah, suppose it is." Jules looked at his friend and the apartment for a long moment. "Things change, though." He paused. "You know why you and me work, Max?" Jules asked as he moved gingerly in the bathroom cleaning himself up and checking his cuts.

"Because I'm this smart guy that most underestimate, not knowing that I come from a pretty tough background and you are this really bright guy that comes from a really tough background?"

Jules smiled at Max.

"Naw, Max, the reason we work is because you are the exact opposite of me. You live in the suburbs. I live in the city. You're a CPA. Me, I am a computer tech at the Tribune. The most unlikely of friends," Jules said.

"Okay," Max said.

"Me, I'm black. You, Max, you're white."

"Okay, I failed at babysitting and now you are going to state all the obvious shit that I should have realized for some reason."

"No, man, I ain't stating the obvious. I am pointing out the things that make us better when we are together. It is our differences. Some of those differences are minor. Some are pretty big."

"Yeah. Yeah, I see that," Max said. "But it is a strength to see those differences."

"I don't know about that. All I know is that I keep my friends separate, generally. I was thinking about that today. I don't let anyone in all the way. I have boundaries."

"We all have boundaries, Jules," Max said.

"Yeah, I suppose."

"Oh, and by the way, you suck at being the strong and silent type."

"Yeah. I definitely do."

There was a natural pause between the two friends.

"Jules, I got to talk with Bethany. I was sort of impressed."

"Why?"

"She's exactly not like anyone I have every introduced you to," Max laughed. "She's nothing like the girls I have made you meet."

Jules nodded.

"So, what's going on?" Max said, rhetorically.

Jules knitted his brows, thinking. He looked at Max and lowered his head. Max had bandaged his forearm expertly. Jules had patched his thigh with gauze and tape.

"You know how I was saying that I block off what my friends know?" He searched for the right words. "Boundaries."

"Yeah," Max answered.

"Well, I don't feel that way with Bethany." Jules paused. "I let you meet her. I want her to meet all my friends. That's never happened."

Max did not respond. He looked at his friend who had bandaged his forearm and tried to understand what he was trying to say without saying it. As friends there was an expected shorthand in communication. Max was tasked with the heavy lifting all of a sudden.

"So, what do we do now?"

"Nothing. Once I patch myself up, we'll go and find Bethany. Maybe we can have a late lunch."

"What? No, Jules, you don't get it. I mean, I'm your friend. I love you. I came over to help you out with Bethany. Like I said, I like her. She didn't tell me much but what she did tell me is not good," Max said frustrated suddenly. "You are mixed up with some Rogers Park drug boy who has come up on the streets and believes he owns that girl of yours."

Jules smiled.

"There's nothing funny here, Jules," Max said.

"The whole thing is squashed, Max," Jules said. "You shouldn't try to sound black. It's embarrassing."

"Squashed?"

"Like a bug on a windshield," Jules smiled.

"So, we ain't worrying about a d-boy trying to hurt you or Bethany?"

Jules shook his head no as he moved out of the small bathroom. "Stop trying to sound all Boyz N the Hood."

"Bethany know about all this?"

"She knows parts. She knows that I went to talk to the d-boy and that I promised to end the whole thing but she's a little skeptical," Jules replied.

"Skeptical?" Max scoffed. "You sure you want to be mixed up with someone like this?"

Jules checked his ear and wasn't surprised that Max had put a cartoon band-aid on it and though it was tender to the touch it was manageable. He smiled at the realization that the shit he was forced to swallow was like the pain in his forearm or thigh, manageable. He walked to his closet to grab a clean pair of jeans and a clean shirt.

"Max, I know how this is going to sound but I bet dollars to donuts I marry that girl," Jules chuckled with a shake of his head.

"What?" Max was stunned. "You can't be serious."

Bandaged and in a clean pair of jeans Jules searched for a T-shirt to wear. He paused and looked at the bandage on his forearm. He found a long sleeve T-shirt. Jules pushed Max out of his bedroom and into the living room.

"Seriously," Jules said. "I have never wanted to move heaven and earth for anyone, but I do for her. I think Bethany is everything that I am looking for in someone that I want to be with."

Jules slipped his long sleeve T-shirt over his head. He was not surprised to see Max on the couch.

Max was stymied. He sat on the overstuffed couch. He sat and looked at Jules dumbfounded.

Jules sat on the couch with Max. He put a hand on his friend's shoulder.

"Max, I asked you to watch my girl until I got back. I wanted you to meet her. She's the real thing, Max. At least, for me," Jules breathed. "I understand that things started crazy. There's nothing wrong with a little crazy. I mean, we all need a little crazy in our lives. But most incredible things seem crazy. In just a handful of days I have realized that all the things that I was afraid of were things that held me back from a life filled with brightness. I have learned so much because of Bethany. I mean, when someone comes along that is good and sweet and makes your heart turn a flip you have to take chances. I don't want to regret not trying to be with her." He paused. "I know that it's scary. I know that it sounds crazy. Hell, love is scary and crazy."

"You saying you love this girl?"

Jules did not respond. He simply smiled, a smile which spread across his face like the thoughts of Bethany.

"So, logic is out the window?" Max decided. "I can't point out that you barely know this girl? I can't mention that she's connected to a Rogers Park d-boy?"

"No," Jules smiled.

"So, when's the wedding date?"

"Huh?" Jules said shocked. "Slow down cowboy. I just said that I plan on marrying her. I need a little time to make sure."

"I'm glad we aren't close to Las Vegas," Max said. "I mean, you would probably elope, if you got a chance."

Jules laughed. "I wouldn't want to spoil the chance to have a bachelor's party with you and Aich and Tre. Now, that would be worth the whole wedding," Jules laughed.

"Aich and Tre scare me more than this Bethany girl," Max said. "I mean, I know they're your friends and all. But they are a little scary."

"They are pussycats."

"Yeah. Sabretooth killer pussycats," Max said.

Jules laughed.

"Seriously, Tre, the shorter one, is like Eazy E from NWA."

"Aich is the shorter one," Jules said. "And the next time I talk to them I am going to tell them that you think they should have been in NWA."

"Come on," Max said.

"I'm just kidding," Jules said.

"Seriously, do not tell them that," Max said.

"You hungry?"

Max shrugged his shoulders.

Jules fished out his phone. He dialed Bethany. After a few rings she answered.

"Bee, where are you?" Jules looked at Max and shook his head. "Bee, you know that I wouldn't leave you with just anyone. Max is my best friend. You can trust him. I know. I don't care." He paused. "Stay there. We're coming."

He hung up and looked at the cowed Max.

"Come on," Jules said. "She's at Paulie Gee's." Jules shook his head. "She wanted deep dish."

The two friends, complete opposites, walked from the apartment to North Milwaukee Avenue and Paulie Gee's.

Paulie Gee's is one of those local pizza spots that attracts all ages but caters to the college crowd. Since the majority of the people walking in were from college everything had a theme. Everything had fancy names.

The music in Paulie Gee's was themed as well. They were playing, when Max and Jules walked in music from the eighties. Depeche Mode was playing "Master and Servant" when the pair arrived. The music was a blend of pop, hip hop and rock. The music was all the hits for the decade.

Paulie Gee's was an active and social hot spot. There was always a crowd at Paulie Gee's at night. At a few minutes to three it was a light crowd. No more than fifty people were seated, talking and eating when Max and Jules arrived. Bethany was sitting at a table with a deep-dish pizza in front of her with three beers, when the Jules and his college friend arrived.

"You expecting someone?"

"Just you and my babysitter," Bethany said.

"So, Bee, you know Max," Jules smiled.

Bethany smiled. "We met."

"Briefly," Max said, looking at Bethany curiously.

"Bee, this is one of my closest friends," Jules said. "I trust him with my life."

"Uh huh," Bethany grunted.

"What's wrong," Jules asked.

"I'm mad at you," Bethany said.

"Why?"

"Think that I'll give you two a little space," Max said and stood up and smiled. Max grabbed a slice of pizza and a napkin and his beer and walked away.

Jules looked at Bethany. Bethany stared at Jules angrily.

Jules watched as Max made his way to the bar and sat with his slice of pizza and beer. Jules smiled at Max. He turned back to Bethany.

Bethany was pouting.

"What's wrong Bee," Jules asked.

"I fell asleep with you by me and woke up with you gone," Bethany said. She was angry.

"I'm sorry," Jules said placing a hand on hers.

She looked up with those gigantic brown eyes and Jules felt the earth shift. He smiled.

"Bee, I promised you that I would protect you. So, I did," Jules said, reaching out and placing his hand on her shoulder. He took his hand from her shoulder and placed her hand in his.

Bethany looked down at Jules giant hand compared to hers and smiled.

"Jules tell me that things are going to be all right," Bethany said.

"Bee, things are going to be all right," Jules said.

Bethany leaned close to Jules. "I was thinking that we could just leave here and not have to deal with Diamond and Rogers Park," Bethany tried. She seemed anxious all of a sudden. It reminded Jules of the first meeting he had with the beautiful Bethany Sullivan.

Jules smiled.

"I'm serious."

"What about your mom, Bee?"

Bethany quieted. She looked down, uncertain. Jules reached out and gently lifted her head with his thumb and forefinger.

"I solved the whole situation," Jules said. "Everything is like I said on the text. You got my note, right?"

Bethany nodded.

"We are good. No more worries about Diamond," Jules said. "It's just you and me and tall grass and clover."

"What's that mean?"

He paused.

"No more outside Rogers Park problems," Jules smiled.

"You sure?"

"I'm as sure as I can be," Jules said pulling Bethany close to him and giving her a gentle hug. "Remember I won't lie to you."

"Don't ever leave me like that again," Bethany said.

"Won't have to, Bee," Jules admitted. Jules looked back and saw Max at the end of the bar eating his pizza and watching the couple.

Jules smiled.

"Are we good again?"

Bethany smiled and drew closer to Jules. She reached out and hugged him. It was a bit awkward, the hug, as Jules and Bethany were sitting at a tall round table with Bethany on Jules' right. Jules laughed at the awkward half hug.

"You not going to hug me back?"

Jules twisted and turned and gave Bethany a less awkward hug.

When they separated Jules leaned close to Bethany and gave her the slightest kiss on her cheek. Bethany looked at Jules for a full second to register the kiss, if it was a kiss. The brushing of his lips against her cheek had been more a breath than a kiss.

Bethany smiled up at Jules. Her head was braced by her palm.

"Can I bring Max back over?"

Bethany hesitated.

"What? You don't like Max?"

Bethany did not speak. She just looked at Max at the bar eating and drinking his beer.

"How you know him?"

"I told you," Jules smiled. "College. He was the first person that was nice to me at school."

"You and Max good friends?"

"Yeah, I don't have a ton of friends. I just have people that I work with, people I grew up with and Max."

Bethany listened.

Jules signaled for Max to return.

Bethany smiled. "He's nice. Odd, but nice."

The music changed and suddenly there was a bunch of oohs and ahhs as Montel Jordan's "This Is How We Do It" oozed out of the speakers. The small lunch crowd started singing along.

"That's my boy," Jules said gesturing for Max to return. "I trust him with my wife, Bee."

Bethany narrowed her eyes not sure if she heard Jules correctly.

Jules gestured again to Max and Max returned with just his beer.

"Jules, what did you say?"

"Hey, thanks for inviting me to lunch," Max said. "I think there might be another lunch waiting at the apartment when you return. I did order some food earlier."

Bethany tried to get Jules' attention.

Jules pretended not to hear Bethany as Max sat and took the second beer.

Max and Jules ate like Jules ate; Bethany noticed. The beauty grabbed a slice of pizza as the two eaters ate slice after slice of pizza.

Jules slowed eating, after his second slice and noticed the pizza still tasted the same even after Rogers Park. He looked at the high round table and it was no different than the last time Jules had been at Paulie Gee's. Jules climbed to his feet and reached out and hugged Bethany and, in his arms, she smiled. Jules looked around Paulie Gee's and studied the walls and the people and noticed the sky, the sidewalk, the cars, the apartment, Max and everything around him things had not changed either since his fight with Diamond.

"Jules, what are you doing?"

"I'm just looking at things, Bee," Jules smiled. "Just looking at things, differently."

"Not too differently," Bethany said.

"No, not too differently," Jules said finding Max looking at Bethany and Jules hugged up together.

Max twisted his thin lips beneath his straight, thin nose and smiled at Jules and Bethany. Max had a slice of pizza in hand and stopped himself from inhaling it. He smiled broadly and took a deep sip of the beer he had been nursing since his return to the table.

"I know when I've become a third wheel," Max said.

Bethany seemed surprised at Max's words. Jules simply smiled and nodded.

"No, Max, you don't have to leave," Bethany said.

Jules smiled.

"I have a wife and a daughter who might disagree with you, on that one," Max laughed.

Max climbed to his feet, fished out his wallet, and tried to calculate his damage. He threw down a twenty and bowed. "Bethany, hope to see more of you. Treat my boy right. He deserves a break.

You look like good people." Max turned to go. He leaned in and whispered to Jules: "I think you're right. She looks like someone worth fighting for. Good choice. Remember that I made you go to the club to meet her."

Jules clapped Max on the back and the two college friends hugged. Max left Bethany and Jules to the nineties classic "...Baby One More Time." Jules chortled as Bethany and he sat in Paulie Gee's.

"I like Max," Bethany laughed after Max had left and Jules and he had hugged before Max returned to his home. "I don't usually like guys like him."

"Like I said, he's good people," Jules nodded. He added, "Always nice to have one in case I go somewhere that might involve police."

Bethany smiled at Jules' joke.

Jules smirked. He tried not to smile too much. Jules was sipping a bottled juice. He had not drank the beer. He noted that Bethany had a beer.

"How long have you known him?"

"Since school. So, nearly five or six years. He has an adorable wife named: Lorraine and a daughter named: Halle. We have to go out and see them. You'd love them. Halle is the sweetest. I think she's four now. They are good people. Even if they live in Oak Park." Jules paused and chuckled.

"What's funny?"

"I don't know," Jules said. "Today, started out just like any other day and now I'm here with you. I got some good people in my life. I just was thinking that I surround myself with good people."

Bethany nodded her approval. She was looking at the pizza box that was still on the table in front of them. Max's twenty-dollar bill was sitting on top of the carton. Bethany looked up and studied Jules.

"What?" Jules smiled. He could not stop smiling at Bethany. She possessed the biggest and deepest brown eyes. Her straight brown nose sat above her incredibly luscious lips. Jules smiled as Bethany smiled to reveal her singular dimple.

"You want anything else?"

Bethany looked at Jules questioningly.

"Jules," Bethany began.

"Ice cream? Cake?"

"Jules," Bethany said annoyed at Jules pushing back her question. She pouted for some reason. Bethany sulked.

Jules looked and noted for the first time that Bethany was not smiling beside him. He gave Bethany his undivided attention.

"Bee, what's wrong?"

"You are playing and I'm trying to be serious."

"Serious? About what?"

Bethany was annoyed but even in her annoyance Jules could not help but smile at her grace and preciousness. Bethany tried to frown but as Jules smiled Bethany's frown cracked. The attempt to stay angry was fleeting. Bethany smiled because Jules smiled.

"Yes," Jules smiled and reached out to hold Bethany's hand. Bethany smiled with Jules' gentle touch.

"What did I hear you say earlier?"

Jules smiled, feigning ignorance. He looked at Bethany who was suddenly very serious but still incredibly cute.

"What did you hear me say earlier?" Jules looked at the girl with the heart shaped face and tilted his head to the left to look at Bethany from a different angle.

"Do you remember what you said to me about Max?"

Jules smiled. He tilted his head to the right and smiled.

"I said a lot to Max about you," Jules said.

"No," Bethany said getting annoyed. "About Max and me and trust."

Jules smiled.

"Something about trusting Max with your wife?"

"You sure you heard me say that?" Jules joked playfully. He was studying Bethany like a teenager. "Or was that wishful thinking?"

"Jules," Bethany said seriously. She narrowed her big brown eyes.

The Spice Girls "Wannabe" started to play.

"I like this song," Jules confessed. Jules looked around and enjoyed the new energy which arose because of the Spice Girls.

Jules climbed off his chair and hugged Bethany. Bethany smiled despite her protests.

"Remember when we met at the club and you asked me if I danced?"

Bethany smiled. She nodded.

"Well, this is me bar dancing," Jules said shaking his booty and moving his shoulders robotically. Bethany shook her head at the sight of Jules dancing. Well, bar dancing.

"Jules, stop playing around." Bethany pinched her lips. She smiled despite herself. Bethany smiled at the man in front of her. Jules in a long-sleeve T-shirt and jeans dancing like...she did not know.

"Yes, my love," Jules confessed. Jules smiled with the confession. He watched Bethany's eyes widen.

"Yes, my love?" Bethany slowly repeated.

"Yes, my love," Jules repeated. "I told you I wouldn't lie to you."

Bethany opened and closed her mouth. She studied Jules. She opened her mouth, but no words came out. She closed her mouth.

Jules smiled and studied Bethany. Paulie Gee's looked as it had before. There was no brighter greens, oranges, yellows, reds or blues. Yet, as he looked at Bethany wearing her light blue blouse her skin seemed to be filled with the brightness of the sun. Jules looked at Bethany and took all of her beauty in, like a breath of fresh air. He looked down and marveled at the size disparity between his hand and hers.

He looked up and into her heart shaped face, framed by her Afro puffs. Her dark eyebrows trembled. Jules looked at Bethany and saw a single tear race along her honey dipped cheek.

Jules' hand caught the tear against Bethany's cheek. He held her cheek gently there in Paulie Gee's as she reached out and hugged the man who proclaimed he loved her. He held her and let her rest against his chest.